MW01144198

A Pathway to Survival

Kari Martinez

PublishAmerica
Baltimore

ISBN: 1-4241-8044-9
PUBLISHED BY PUBLISHAMERICA, LLLP
www.publishamerica.com
Baltimore

Printed in the United States of America

I dedicate this book first to my daughter. She has given me more strength than anyone could imagine. I also dedicate this book to all the people who have helped me along the way. To my therapist who helped me realize that the choices I made were not wrong. To the people in group therapy who helped me realize I was not alone. They have all provided me with the knowledge to help me to truly survive. Special thanks to my family for their love.

Introduction

This story is about rape, feelings, failures, and the struggle to survive. The contents of this book may stir up feelings and emotions for any person that has been raped or sexually abused.

By telling this story that it will inspire others to seek the help they deserve. Also, let people know whether or not the rape was reported does not change anything. Everyone has a right to survive. They have a right to have a life. Even, if they are not believed. They are the only one that can deal with what happened to them. The only person that needs to know the truth is the victim. What other people think does not matter. Even though there will be times that you will feel the need to have people believe you.

Being a survivor is not just about surviving that moment. It is about the survival of everything that follows. Living through that night and going on and existing. Not just going through life trying to forget that night ever happened and needing to go through the steps of healing. Without going through the steps can you really be a true survivor. Basically, to survive the sexual assault does not end at the moment the act is over. That one act will live with you for the rest of your life. You can try to hide it, but it will always come back. It will always be there until you actually deal with the pain, shame, fears, and failures from that one moment. Those feelings can go away with hard work. The fact that people survive their attacker is the first step to healing. The next step is being ready to deal with those feelings. Excepting that you can not change what happened. Except that it is not your fault. The decisions you make are not wrong. No matter what choices made he has no right to do what he did. Needing someone to blame is a normal response. Blaming yourself is normal. Having the need to be punished for what happen is normal. The worst thing is blaming yourself for failing. After that moment every time you believe you failed at something it makes things worse. You feel a need to achieve at a higher level. If you don't then you feel as if you failed all over again. As you read this story, you will know what was perceived to be failure.

No matter how long ago the rape happened, no matter what happened, no matter how it happened, and no matter where it happened, the story inside can be told and the pain, shame, guilt, fear, and other thousands of emotions can be released and you can heal.

You never think you will get over what happened. Know you will never forget what happened. Learning how to deal with the emotions from that night is so important. Forgive yourself for the choices and let go of the failure you feel. Each struggle to heal, in itself, is a journey. I truly believe that everyone is a survivor. They have the strength to survive the sexual abuse, and they have the strength to survive the healing process.

Nobody can tell you what to do to survive. That has to be your choice, and on your terms. Nobody can force you before you are ready. You cannot force yourself to go through those steps. You have to be ready to take on the challenges that you will have to face. At times you will want to speed up the healing process. It will not go any faster than what your mind and body will allow. Your mind knows what you can handle at every stage of the healing process. Different stages will become more difficult and you will want to quit. You will want to go back to what made you feel comfortable, maybe even try to run and hide. Different things will happen to keep you going to help you through those difficult times. The mind and body know what it could handle. It gives us what we needed for each step of the healing process. The journey is worth the pain and struggle. Without feeling those emotions they will never go away. Brining those emotions back and dealing with those feelings is one of the hardest things any person can go through. At times you won't believe that you will make it through the healing process, finding the strength you needed to make it through. Strength can and will come from several different places. Sometimes what you perceived as strength from people around you is really those feelings of failure. Be glad every day that the strength is with you.

Chapter 1

Sandy was a young girl attending college at a small liberal arts school in the Midwest. It was the spring semester of her freshman year. It was around 2:00 a.m. Sandy had been in the gym, working out. Sandy knew it was late and that she needed to get back to the dorm. She finished working out and left. She exited the building. She could see the streetlights and outside lights on the main classroom building. In the distance, she could see the lights to the dorm entrance across the street. The night air was cool; she had left her jacket back at her dorm room. She was wearing sweat pants and a T-shirt.

She had gone to the gym earlier that afternoon after track practice. It was a nice warm spring day. She shut the door behind her. She wrapped her arms around her chest to stay warm. As she walked down the stairs to the sidewalk, she rubbed her hands together blowing on them as if it would keep her warm. She walked past the main building, and she started past the library. There was a man standing by the northwest corner of the library.

She thought nothing of him standing there. She wasn't afraid or nervous about walking by him. It was cold and all she cared about was getting back to the dorm. She wanted to take a nice hot shower to warm up.

Sandy walked toward the man and glanced over at him. She made eye contact and acknowledged his presence, and continued past him. She had taken only a few steps past him. She felt an arm around her shoulders and throat and a hand over her mouth. He picked her up off the ground and carried her to the west side of the library behind the bushes. He pushed her up against the wall with one hand over her mouth and the other on her throat. Her back was against the wall, and her feet barely touching the ground. He looked into her eyes, and leaned close to her face and in a very soft voice told her not to scream or move. It was almost as if he was whispering, trying not to disturb the person next to him. She stood there like a stone, moving only her eyes, trying to look around, looking into his eyes, hoping this was not real. After a few seconds she started to squirm. Sandy tried to push him away. He held onto her throat even tighter, shoving her head against the building. In a quiet, stern voice he ordered her to stop moving. When she wouldn't, he grabbed her by the shoulders and threw her to the ground. He put his hand back on her mouth, pushing her head into the stones. He sat straddling her stomach and chest. Leaving her left arm free, she was able to hit him a couple of times. He grabbed her left arm. He brought up his right knee and placed it on the upper part of her arm. He pulled her arm above her head. Her mind was racing with thoughts and questions. Her body was now panicking and trembling from fear. She forgot about the cold night air. It no longer seemed cold.

He grabbed her right arm from under his leg and put it above her head on top of her left arm. He grabbed her wrist with his other hand. Now his legs were squeezing her from her ribs to her hips keeping her still. He looked down at her and told her again in a stern voice don't you "scream, 'cause no one is gonna hear you."

She started looking around. She could see the lights of the street and a glimmer of light from the dorm entrance. She was so close to home. She was so close to being safe and warm. Yet she was too far away to reach the dorm. She could not hear anyone, or see anyone. The only sound she heard was from the cars going down the main street. The main street was about one hundred yards from the front of the building. Nobody would hear a sound.

He took his hand from her mouth. She did not scream. He sat on her stomach and chest with one hand, and he unzipped his pants with the other, causing him to loosen the grip from her wrists. Sandy was able to get her hands free. With all the strength she had she started to hit him in his chest and back. He grabbed the top of her head, pulling her hair. He lifted her head off the ground and began to pound her head down on the rocks. As she stopped struggling from the pain she was feeling, he grabbed both her hands again, locking one hand around both her wrists. He rolled her over slightly onto her left side. He placed her right arm behind her back and rolled her back so she was lying on top of her arm. She could no longer move her arm. He took her left arm and placed it back over her head. She tried to pull her arm away. He used his left hand to hold it down. He finished unzipping his pants. He reached into his pants and grabbed his penis. He slid down her body until he was lying on top of her.

He told her again to stop moving. After he laid down on top of her, he grabbed her chin, squeezing as he spoke. He whispered to her. "Don't move." He took his hand away from her chin. He reached down to pull down her sweat pants and underwear. He was unable to get them off, so he began rolling her from side to side. Each time he moved her to the right it put more pressure on her right arm. When he would move her to her left side, it released some of the pressure from her arm. After a few times she realized that each time he moved her to the left she was able to move her arm a little. Sandy tried to move her arm out from under her. When he got her pants and underwear down by her knees, he stopped rolling her. She was unable to completely free her arm. He took his hand and started to rub her vagina. She continued to try and get her arm free.

He was gentle at first. He rubbed the surface with the palm of his hand. He slowly moved his hand up and down. He started to barely push his finger in her vagina. The feeling was soft and gentle. Her body was enjoying the feeling that came from what he was doing. Body sensations were sparked. As he felt her body responding, he rubbed harder. It became painful. He asked her how it felt. She did not respond to his question. She couldn't answer his questions; she didn't know how it felt. She was scared. She didn't know how or what it should have felt like. It made him angry. He took his hand away from rubbing her. He grabbed her chin to force her to answer him.

She told him, "No."

He was trying to force her to answer. He released her left arm. She started to hit him and squirm, trying to get him off of her. He became angry. The more she moved and fought, the more intense his anger grew. He got up and sat on her stomach and chest with all his weight. It made it hard for her to breathe. It felt like she was being crushed. She could only take in short, shallow breaths. He slapped her across the face, one right after the other. Sandy kept moving, trying desperately to get away. The fear and panic she was feeling were more powerful than anything else she was feeling at that moment, she wanted to get up and run as fast as she could. When he realized that she was not going to stop, he grabbed the top of her head with one hand. Her grabbed her chin with the other and picked her head up and slam it into the rocks. When she stopped moving, he stopped slamming her head down. She was in a fog. She felt numb all over. The numbness of her body and the fog she was feeling took all her energy at that moment.

She started to wonder what would happen. What was he going to do? Would she die? Would he let her go? At that moment, she was hoping and praying to die. The cool night air, the panic, the fear, the desire to die, and thousands of other thoughts ran through her head. She was no longer able to move. She could feel what was going on, she could see bits and pieces, but she couldn't seem to move any more. She was frozen in that moment.

He grabbed her chin, she looked into his face, and he told her, "Now your not gonna move."

She didn't move. She just lay there. He started to kiss her. She moved her head side to side. She moved her head side to side each time he would try to kiss her and stick his tongue down her throat. She was moving her head away from the shame and fear. She started to hide at that moment. That was the moment when she lost everything. That was the moment she knew her life was over. Either she was going to die or she was going to no longer be the same person.

He grabbed her T-shirt between his teeth and ripped it down to her stomach. He then took her bra in his mouth and did the same thing; the bra was harder to tear. The thick seams made it harder to rip apart. He placed his hands over her breasts, rubbing and squeezing. He moved from one breast to the other. Sometimes he would try and squeeze them together. He used his tongue and licked her breasts. Moving his mouth around her nipples and then covering her nipples with his mouth. Sucking and grabbing them in his teeth. His teeth felt sharp. It hurt every time he put the nipples in his teeth and pulled. It felt like his teeth were cutting her. Her nipples grew hard her body felt a tingling sensation. It was not the same tingling she felt when her head hit the ground. This tingling was from the pleasure her body was feeling. The shimmering and tingle went down her entire body. She could not understand why her body was reacting to what was happening, how it could betray her. Having a sense of pleasure with what was happening to her at that moment. She could not control her body's reaction. With one hand he would rub her breasts and lick them. With his other hand he rubbed her vagina and stuck his fingers inside her. Every so often he would stop licking her breast. He licked his hands and fingers after being inside her. He told her that she taste good.

He reached into his pants and took out his penis, and grabbed her hand and told her to touch it. She tried to pull away; she did not want to touch him. She did not want him touching her! He licked the palm of her hand and told her to rub him. Sandy couldn't allow herself to rub him. Her body had already betrayed her, with its reaction, how could she let it continue. He wrapped her hand, and fingers around his penis, with his hand on top of hers, he began moving her hand with his up and down. His penis was hard; it felt like it was pulsating in her hand. Her hand reached around her thumb and fingers overlapping. She didn't know how long he made her rub him. When her hand moved up and down she could feel it throbbing and the blood rushing through his penis. He took his hand away. He went back to rubbing her vagina. He put his fingers in her. Shoving his hand in as far as it could go. She let her hand fall from his penis. As he moved his hand in and out of her, the pain was unbelievable. She wanted to scream, the pain was so bad. Other times it was gentle and soft, and her body would enjoy the feeling. She could feel something running out of her. She didn't know what it was. He would say, "See, you like it", or "Doesn't that feel good?" every time she would cum. He finished playing with her vagina and her breast. The pain stopped.

He rolled on top of her. She tried to push him off and she tried to get him to stop. He slapped her again, and told her to stop moving and said she would enjoy this even more. He grabbed his penis with his hand and shoved it in her vagina, keeping his hand there, making sure he went in. When he took his hand away, he shoved his penis in even further. The pain was nothing like she had ever felt before. It hurt going in, but yet it also felt normal. It felt like he had to force his penis into her. The feeling scared her and she began to struggle. She got her right arm free and she pushed and hit him with both hands. He got up to sit on her. She felt relief from the pain. He tried to grab her hands. He couldn't grab both of her hands at the same time, so he grabbed her hair and pulled her head up and pounded it into the rocks again. Her body went limp after the second or third time. An overwhelming pain came over her. She could feel what was happening. She could feel him putting his penis inside her again. She could feel him on top of her. Her body was completely numb.

Sandy was unable to open her eyes and she no longer knew what was happening. The next thing she remembered was trying to open her eyes. It hurt when she tried. She was squinting to see what was happening. Her eyelids felt heavy. Her head was swimming in the cloudiness surrounding her body. She knew she was still on the ground, but she no longer knew exactly what was happening. When it felt as if the fog lifted she was able to pick up her arms. She reached to hold the back of her head with her hand as she was lifting her head up. She could feel the wetness from her hair. She rubbed the back of her head. She opened her eyes. She finally was able to sit up. She brushed herself, trying to wipe the dirt off. She tried to stand for the first time. She didn't make it to her feet. She tried leaning against the building and slid down to the ground. She sat against the building. She wasn't ready to pick herself up. She looked around. It was dark.

She could still see the lights glimmering from the dorm entrance. Her pants and underwear were around her right leg. He had taken everything off her left leg. She felt this calmness over her, like nothing was real. She pulled her underwear and pants on. She looked around for her shoe. She reached for her shoe, stretching out to reach her shoe, and trying not to fall over when she grabbed it. She grabbed her shoe to put in on. She looked down and her breasts were showing. It was getting colder as the morning went on. She pulled her shirt around her, holding it together with one hand. She tried pulling herself up off the ground leaning on the side of the building. She finally made it to her feet. She walked against the wall, stumbling through the bushes. Back to where it all started, she walked toward the light of the dorm taking each step hoping not to fall. She reached into her pocket to get her key to unlock the door. She walked to the stairs to go up to her room. Each step she took was a struggle to hang on. She felt weak; her muscle felt tight, she hurt in places she never knew could hurt. Sandy made it to her room and she sat on the edge of the bed.

Her roommates were gone. One was at the sorority house, the other was with her boyfriend. She sat for a while to rest. She walked to the dresser, pulled out a clean T-shirt and put it on. Sandy picked herself up off the bed and proceeded downstairs. It was easier going down than it was going up. Sandy held onto the rail so not to fall. Sandy stopped and sat on the step when she felt dizzy and couldn't go on any further. The pain increased with every move she made. Sandy reached the lobby where the resident assistant sat every night. The RA was sitting at the desk. Sandy stumbled on the last step. The resident assistant on duty saw her stumble and went over to help her. The RA grabbed her arm and took her into the RA room. The RA had her sit on the couch and put a pillow behind her head and a blanket over her to give her comfort and keep her warm.

The RA called the police. She was numb, she was cold, she couldn't think, she was tired, she hurt all over, she wanted to sleep, and the R.A. tried to hand her the phone. She couldn't talk to anyone; she pushed the blanket off of her. She tried to stand herself up from the sofa. Once she was on her feet she walked out of the room, it was a struggle to walk back to her room, hanging onto the railing, pulling herself up each step of the way. She finally reached her room. Sandy sat down in a chair by the desk. Sandy opened the drawer to grab clothes and pulled herself up from the chair with the help of the desk. Sandy grabbed all the clothes she had on the floor and took them with her to the bathroom. Sandy walked into the bathroom. It was difficult to take her clothes off for a shower. Leaning against the wall, taking off her T-shirt, pulling it above her head, the pain in her arms was unreal. Pushing down her sweat pants, she could see blood on her legs, and on her clothes. The pain was almost unbearable as she leaned against the wall and saw all the blood. Sandy began to feel dizzy. Sandy sat on the floor for a few minutes to get herself steadied.

When she got up to go in the shower, she stood holding the wall with her body, trying not to fall over. She turned on the water. It was cold at first. When the water became warmer, she sat down on the shower floor. The water ran over her, when she looked down she could see the blood, dirt, debris, and the water run down the drain. She leaned her head against the wall, Sandy closed her eyes, and her mind drifted away. The shower started to get cold. She started to shiver from being cold all over again. She crawled out of the shower, pulled herself up on the bench with her clothes. Sandy grabbed her towel and dried off as best she could. She reached for her clothes to put them on. When she finished dressing, she grabbed the clothes off the floor and wadded them up in her arms. She stood up and pulled the curtain back and walked out of the shower. She left the bathroom and dropped her clothes into the trash can. She walked back to her room, holding onto the wall so she wouldn't fall over. She reached her bed and crawled in, pulling the blankets over her, covering her head as if she was freezing cold and trying to get warm. She didn't know how long she was in bed. Sandy didn't even really know what had happened in that time period. She just couldn't get out of bed. She couldn't move. She wanted to stay there forever. She felt so ashamed. She felt like a complete failure. She felt that she should have prevented this from happening. She was worthless.

This was her fault. Sandy should have been more careful. Sandy should have not been walking alone at night. Sandy should have taken a different way home. Sandy should have called someone to walk her home. Why did she stay so late in the gym? Sandy should have gone home earlier. *Why? Why? Why?* kept going through her mind. There was no way around it, it was her fault and she had no one to blame but herself. Because she was stupid, this was her punishment for not being smart enough or strong enough to have done things differently.

Chapter 2

Finally, Sandy got out of bed. Her head and body ached. It felt like she pulled every muscle in her body. Sandy had bruises on her arms, more on her right arm than her left. Her roommates were surprised to see her; they had tried to get her out of bed for days to go to classes, but she wouldn't get up. They told her she said to leave her alone. Sandy didn't feel good, so they did. After a few minutes of talking to one of her roommates, Sandy grabbed some clothes from the dresser and went to take a shower. When she had finished with her shower, they asked her if she was going down for breakfast with the rest of them. Sandy still hurt. Sandy grabbed some ibuprofen to take with breakfast. Part of her felt like she had partied way too hard, and was so drunk that she passed out. Another part felt like she had been in a fight with a bulldozer and lost.

The RA came up to Sandy at breakfast and asked to talk to her in the apartment. She asked Sandy how she was doing. Sandy told her that she was a little tired and sore, but okay. She took Sandy into the apartment and sat her down on the sofa where Sandy had been a few nights before. The R.A. told Sandy that she should go see the school counselor. She called and made an appointment for Sandy that afternoon. Sandy didn't understand why she wanted her to see the counselor. Sandy went that afternoon and met with the counselor, who appeared to be nice. Sandy sat in a chair. They stared at each other for what seemed like for ever. After a while, the counselor asked Sandy questions about classes and her roommates, how things were going. As the counselor asked the questions, the phone rang. She answered the call and spent a few minutes on the phone. The phone rang about three more times during the first visit. She answered the phone every time. Sandy hated the fact the phone would ring and she would answer it, even though she would not talk long, it was annoying. Sandy wondered how she could talk to anyone with the phone ringing all the time. Sandy only saw the school counselor twice. They never talked about anything other than school.

Later that night, Sandy called home. The phone just rang every time she tried calling. Sandy knew her family was home. They were never on the phone very long. Sandy's younger bother and sister would have been home from school. Sandy called late in the evening, late enough that if they had practice or a game they would be home by now. When she couldn't get through, Sandy called a friend of the family and asked if she had talked to her mom. Sandy told her she couldn't get through on the phone, and wanted to know if she knew if their phone was out. Sandy started to cry a little. Sandy needed to reach her mom. Sandy wanted to go home. She held back the tears.

The next day the family friend drove to her parents' house to tell them she was trying to reach them. The next day Sandy's mom called told her the lines had been out for a couple of days. Sandy's mom seamed kind of upset. Calling the family friend seemed like a lot to go through to go home for the weekend. The family friend did not mind. She was very kind and considerate. She was kind of like a second mom to Sandy. Sandy always knew that she could call and ask her for anything and she would do what she could to help.

School was almost out for the summer. Only a few weeks left. That Friday night, Sandy's mom came and picked her up at school. On the way home Sandy slept in the passenger seat, waking up when the car would slow down or stop. That weekend Sandy kept to herself. She spent time with the family dog, T. J. He was a terrier mix. Sandy talked to him and she would cry every now and then. Sandy always stopped herself because she felt she shouldn't cry. Sandy didn't remember much about that weekend other than she didn't want to go back to school. Her parents gave her one of the cars so she could come home right after finals since the school year was almost over. Sandy didn't tell them anything.

Classes were over, finals had started. Sandy's last final was on Friday morning. Sandy left Friday afternoon and she had everything packed and ready to go for days. On the drive home all she could think about was finding a job and hanging out with friends from high school. Sandy found a job. She had a few days off each week. She always made sure she had time to run each day and do some type of physical workout. Sandy wanted to go out and have fun again. Sandy would go to the drive-in, watch movies, go to bars, pick up guys, spend time at the amusement park riding roller coasters, lay on the beach and swim in the lake. Summer went on as nothing was different. It was the same thing over and over; work, go out, sometimes stay out all night, go home and sleep for a while, then start all over again.

In June, Sandy was in a car accident. The other car left the scene. Sandy had hurt her foot and was lucky it was only a sprain. Sandy was grateful it was not more serious because school was starting in a couple of months. Sandy needed to keep in shape for the upcoming basketball season.

At the end of July beginning of August, she went to visit relatives for two weeks. Sandy didn't have much fun on that trip. Sandy stayed away from most people. Sandy didn't really want to hang out with family. Everyone seemed different; aunts, uncles, and cousins. It seemed that everyone was different. Sandy went to the school by her grandmother's house and ran on the track every day. Sometimes she would also take a basketball and shoot hoops for a while. Sandy was glad when the vacation over. She was ready to go back home and get ready for school to start. Sandy transferred to a new college. She wanted to start over. Classes did not begin until September. Sandy's birthday was at the end of August. Sandy went to her old college to visit with friends and hang out for her birthday. They went to the usual hang out across the street from the campus. They ate dinner and had a few drinks. Sandy did not want to go on campus, to the dorms, or past the library. They sat for several hours, talking drinking and catching up from the summer. It was getting late they asked Sandy if she wanted to stay. It was about 1:30 a.m. when Sandy decided it was time to go. Her car was sitting right outside. Sandy told her friends that she needed to get home. She had to finish packing. Sandy was moving into the dorm that weekend. They said their goodbyes and Sandy got in the car and started back home. The drive was about an hour and a half. When Sandy got on the open road she went as fast as she could. When she reached the towns, Sandy would slow down. Sandy got home about 2:30 a.m. She sat and watched TV for a while, then went to bed around 3:30 a.m. Sandy had to be at work by 5:30 a.m. Sandy didn't sleep much anymore. Sometimes she didn't sleep at all. Other nights she slept for only a few hours at a time. During the day, if she had a few hours, she napped in the living room on the couch.

Chapter 3

Classes started in early September. The first week of school was scary and exciting. Sandy was scared because she didn't know anyone. All the friends she made were back at the old school. Sandy had a new roommate for a few days. Her roommate was a sophomore. Her roommate had her own friends whom she hung out with. This left Sandy all alone. Sandy had no one. No roommate. Sandy was all by herself, starting over in a new school. The campus was nice. There was so much available for students to do. Sandy had met with the basketball and track coaches. Sandy started a workout program. Sandy's routine consisted of running twenty miles a day, lifting weights three times a week, and playing basketball three to four nights a week for about an hour. She would then go back to the dorm and do homework for the rest of the evening. No TV. Sandy would try to go to bed about midnight. Sandy didn't sleep most nights. Sandy just laid in bed thinking about starting over again the next day. Sometimes if homework was light, Sandy would go to the common room and get in on a game of Euchre or pool. Sandy would go to all the dorm meetings, even if attendance wasn't required. Sandy didn't have any friends. Sandy talked to other girls on the floor. Sandy also talked to a few guys on the other floors, but no one she was really close to or could really talk with about what she was going through.

After a few weeks into the semester something strange was happening to Sandy. Sandy didn't know what it was. Sandy was gaining weight and hardly ever had periods since she was always working out lifting weights, running, and playing basketball. Somehow, Sandy knew that she was pregnant, somehow she knew, but what she couldn't figure out was how. Sandy didn't have a boyfriend, she hadn't dated in over a year, and she had never had sex before.

Sandy found a private doctor off campus and went in to see him. Sandy had her first pap smear. He told Sandy she was pregnant. Sandy told him he was wrong. Sandy had never had sex. He ran some tests, and told her how far along she was. Sandy did not hear a word he said. Two days later his office called to tell her that she had gonorrhea and that she needed to tell them who her sex partners were, so they could get treated. Sandy insisted to the nurse that she had no partners and that they must have the wrong person. The nurse scheduled an appointment with Sandy to follow up the next day after classes. After getting off the phone, Sandy went for a run. Sandy ran harder and faster than she had ever run before. Every once in a while she began to cry. As soon as Sandy felt the tears, she forced herself to stop. Sandy didn't want to go back. Sandy wanted to keep running. Sandy got back to the dorm just before night started to fall. Sandy got into her car and went for a drive. Sandy drove around and again she would start to cry, always stopping herself before the tears would come. Sandy didn't know where she was going or what she was going to do. Part of her knew that she was pregnant, part of her knew how it happened, but the other part could not admit it. It was late by the time Sandy got back to the dorm. Sandy tried to go to bed, but she couldn't sleep. Her roommate had moved out a week earlier to stay in a different dorm with her friends. Sandy was completely isolated.

Sandy laid in bed with her hands over her face, holding back the tears. Crying seemed to be all she could do that day. Sandy couldn't allow herself to cry. Sandy wouldn't allow herself to cry. Sandy got up walked down the hall to the bathroom. The RA's door was open. Sandy tapped on the door, and said hi. The RA asked what Sandy was doing up. Sandy told her she couldn't sleep.

The RA looked up from her work. The RA noticed Sandy was upset and that she had been crying. The RA asked Sandy to come in and sit down. The RA was sitting in a chair. Sandy walked in and sat on the couch. She asked Sandy how things were going. Sandy told her everything was fine. She asked about Sandy's classes. Sandy told her they were fine. Sandy asked her how her student teaching was going. She said she had a lot of papers to grade. She said she needed a break. Sandy sat on the couch as she talked. She asked Sandy questions every now and then. After listening to her talk for a while, Sandy started to cry again. Sandy tried to stop. It was harder that time. Sandy stopped the tears once again. The RA got up from her chair and closed the door. She grabbed some tissues and handed it to Sandy and sat back down. Sandy wiped the tears from her face. She asked Sandy what was wrong. Sandy didn't want to tell her. Sandy didn't want anyone to know. The tears started again. Sandy broke down and said she was pregnant. She asked Sandy if she told her boyfriend. Sandy told her that she didn't have a boyfriend. Sandy hadn't dated anyone in over a year. Sandy told her she was raped. She reached over to touch Sandy. Sandy pulled away. She asked Sandy what she was going to do. Sandy told her she didn't know.

Sandy had no idea what was going to happen. Sandy was so lost and confused. Sandy hadn't thought about what to do. Sandy was so busy trying to convince herself that the doctor was wrong, that there was no way she could be pregnant. By telling her and saying it out loud, Sandy knew it was true. Everything that happened over the past few days became real. The reality of what happened in the spring and what was happening now hit her like a ton of bricks. There was no longer denying what happened. Sandy knew now she had some decisions to make.

After a while Sandy got up and left her room. Sandy went to the bathroom. She splashed some water on her face. Sandy grabbed some paper towels to dry herself off. Sandy went back to her room and laid in bed until it was time to get dressed for classes.

The next day, Sandy took her shower and went to classes. The day went by slow at times, other times seemed to move quickly. It was time to go to the doctor's office. Sandy arrived at the doctor's office. Sandy went in and sat down until she was called. They put her in a small room with an exam table. Sandy waited what felt like forever. Finally, the doctor came in. Sandy sat in the chair and she was afraid of what he was going to tell her. He told Sandy that she had a sexually transmitted disease and that she was pregnant and that the baby would be born sometime in January. He wanted Sandy to go for an ultrasound the next day. He handed her a prescription for antibiotics, prenatal vitamins, and scheduled the ultrasound. Sandy told the doctor that she did not want the baby. Sandy told him she wanted an abortion. All she wanted to do was to get rid of the baby. He told Sandy that she was too far along that she could not have an abortion. Sandy may want to try another state, but he did not know because she was so close to the cut-off time. He gave her their name and number. The next morning she called them as soon as they opened. They gave Sandy the cost, but could not guarantee that she could have the abortion. Sandy knew that's what she wanted to do, but she didn't have the money to get there nor any money to pay for an abortion. So Sandy went to classes. She only had a couple of classes that day. Sandy was done before noon. When classes were over, Sandy tried to figure out what she could do, how she could get the money to go and have an abortion. That afternoon Sandy had the ultrasound. After the ultrasound she went back to the dorm. Sandy had to figure out a plan. Sandy called home, spoke to her mom, told a story that she had a medical problem, and needed money to go see this specialist in another state. Sandy's mom told her that she would find a doctor here. Sandy told her that she would get it taken care of and not to worry. So Sandy's mind started to work. How she could hide this from her family and friends. Sandy knew the abortion was out of the question with no money.

As time went on, Sandy ran every night to think about what to do. She would go through each day as if nothing had changed. The next doctor visit, Sandy asked him if he could find a family to adopt the baby. Sandy did not want it. He told Sandy that he could not since she had the sexually transmitted disease. He gave Sandy the number to the welfare office. Sandy contacted them; they said that they could get the baby adopted. They had Sandy come down and fill out paperwork. They asked Sandy all kinds of questions as to the type of family she wanted, religion, background, location of the child, and if she wanted any money. All Sandy wanted was for the medical bills to be covered. Sandy did not care who took the child, just as long as she didn't have to deal with it. Sandy didn't want to know anything about the family who would take this child. Sandy did care about the child.

Sandy was called into the housing office a week later. Sandy went to find out what they wanted. Sandy walked into the office and sat down. Sandy was told that the RA told her that she was pregnant, that they were not going to find her a roommate and that they were not going to charge her for a full-size room. Sandy became angry. The director told Sandy not to be angry with the RA, that she had to tell her. Sandy told her that she didn't care if she gave her a roommate. It didn't matter to her. Sandy told her she was not angry that she told her. Sandy was angry because she did not tell her that she was going to tell anyone. Granted, if Sandy had known that the RA had to tell, she probably wouldn't have said anything. She asked Sandy what she was going to do. Sandy told her that she was looking into adoption. She asked when the baby was due. Sandy told her late January. She asked if Sandy needed anything. Sandy told her she was fine. Sandy felt alone. It didn't matter what anyone tried to do. That feeling never went away. For several days Sandy did not speak to the R.A. Sandy was too angry. Sandy felt betrayed. Sandy felt that she could not trust her. The RA would try and speak to Sandy. The first time, Sandy told her that she did not want to talk to her.

The RA started to take responsibility for Sandy. She checked in on her, making sure Sandy was eating. Some mornings if she saw Sandy in the hall she would ask her to go to breakfast. Sandy wasn't big on breakfast. Sandy usually didn't eat breakfast. She told Sandy that she needed to start eating breakfast every day. The baby needed the nourishment. Sandy didn't care about the baby. Some days, Sandy wouldn't even have lunch or diner. To keep her from harassing her, Sandy went to breakfast with her every once in a while. The evenings, Sandy spent running and working out so she wasn't in the dorm enough for her to force her to eat. The mornings were harder. Sandy didn't sleep much anymore. Sandy was usually awake when she was getting ready to leave in the morning.

Sandy was now getting close to the holidays. Sandy's family was expecting her home. Sandy told them that she could not come home for Thanksgiving, that she had to work with the basketball team. That they were staying on campus. Sandy started to feel lonely, so she went home to surprise her family for Thanksgiving dinner. Nobody said anything. Sandy's mom had told them she was having some medical problems and that was why Sandy looked like she had gained weight. Sandy knew this was the last time she would be able to go home until the baby was born.

Sandy had started to have pains and problems with the pregnancy shortly after Thanksgiving. Sandy was in the hospital to stop contractions. Sandy went into labor a couple of times; Sandy hoped the baby would be born soon. Sandy wanted the child to be born. Sandy didn't care if it lived or not. The doctor would not take the baby sooner. Sandy was pumped full of medication each time in the hospital to stop labor. The doctor wanted to wait as long as possible to let the baby develop. The doctor told Sandy to take it easy and rest. Sandy couldn't take it easy. Sandy had to get rid of the pain she was feeling. It was either running or drinking. Sandy decided on running. Sandy was in and out of the hospital several times in the last months of her pregnancy. Sandy did not care if the baby was born early. Sandy didn't want it anyway. The welfare office found a family for her to stay with over Christmas break. Sandy felt alone, even though she had people around her. Sandy did what she could to get the baby to come early. Sandy didn't know how she could survive if she had to wait any longer.

Christmas break was going to be over soon. On December 29, Sandy woke up around 5:30 a.m. with cramping and spotting. At 7:30 a.m. the family Sandy was staying with was just getting out of bed. Sandy showered and dressed before they woke. When the lady finished getting ready for work, she came into the living room where Sandy was sitting. Sandy asked her if she could take her to the hospital. They got into the car. The lady dropped her two kids off at daycare and then took Sandy to the hospital. She stayed with Sandy and called the other social worker handling the adoption. Sandy was in the delivery room by 9:30 a.m. Around 11:15 a.m. the pain was so bad they did an epidural, finally the pain decreased and Sandy was able to relax for a while. Around 4:45 p.m. the pain had increased and the contractions we closer together. By 5:00 p.m. Sandy started pushing. After two or three pushes Sandy passed out. Only the baby's head was out. Sandy woke up a few minutes later. There were two nurses pushing on her stomach and another nurse was behind her holding her up in the seated position. On each contraction, the nurses pushed on Sandy stomach. It was 5:12 p.m. when the baby was born. Sandy laid back down and the baby was placed on her stomach while they clamped and cut the cord. Sandy was in a daze. Sandy could hear the doctor talking to the nurses, telling them to get ready to take her to the OR. The doctor stood and asked Sandy if she wanted him to call anyone. Sandy told him not to call anyone. The rails on the bed were put up and Sandy was on her way to the operating room. Sandy had an ovarian cyst rupture during the delivery and, as a precaution, they wanted the afterbirth to be delivered in the operating room to make sure she did not start hemorrhaging after the afterbirth was delivered. They went in and removed two ovarian cysts.

A couple of hours later, Sandy was back in her room. There were people waiting for her. The social worker and the lady she was staying with. The social worker asked if she could call anyone for her. Sandy told her no. She told

Sandy that she had a baby girl, 5 pounds, 5 ounces, and 21½ inches long. Sandy didn't really care. Then the doctor came in to see how Sandy was doing. Sandy told him that she was okay. He told Sandy that she had to stay in the hospital for a few days because of the cyst rupturing. He wanted to make sure she was okay before she went home. He told Sandy that he could have the nurse bring the baby in if she wanted to see her. He said she was small, but very healthy.

Sandy was happy the baby was born. Sandy did not want to see her. Sandy did not let them bring her to her room. Sandy spent a few days in the hospital. The first day, Sandy spent on high doses of painkillers in and out of consciousness. During this time, Sandy could hear the babies in the nursery crying. Sandy would begin to cry herself. Sandy put her hands over her face and tried to stop the tears from coming. The nurses came in the room to try and get Sandy out of bed. All Sandy wanted was to do was hide. Sandy couldn't face anyone. Sandy didn't want to face anyone. Sandy couldn't face the world. Sandy was afraid of what was going to happen next. Sandy was feeling guilty about everything; giving the baby away, having the baby, and not telling anyone about the baby. The social worker came in and told Sandy they were taking the baby and putting her with a foster family until the adoption process began. The next day Sandy was able to leave the hospital.

At noon Sandy was picked up by the family she was staying with. The lady took Sandy back to her apartment and she went back to work. Sandy went in and packed up her things. Within an hour, Sandy was in her car driving away.

Chapter 4

Sandy was on the road for two days. She didn't know where she was going or what she was going to do. Sandy just had to get away. Sandy couldn't afford hotel rooms so she slept in her car at rest areas, waiting, hoping, and praying for something to happen, hoping this nightmare was over. Nothing happened. Sandy finally found herself at home. That day she spent as little time as she could with her family, with it being the holidays it was difficult because everyone was home. Sandy spent most of the day in her room with the dog. Sandy couldn't wait for school to start. Sandy wanted to throw herself back into school. Everyone else went to bed. Sandy got up and sat in the living room with the TV on. Sandy began to cry. She was very angry with herself for what had happened. Sandy didn't know how to handle what she was feeling. Sandy sat that night going through everything and by the time morning came she was still confused and upset. It was early that morning, around 7:00 a.m., and Sandy hadn't slept. Sandy walked into her parent's room.

Sandy woke her mom up and told her that she had been raped. Sandy told her mom about the baby girl. Sandy began to cry again and told her mom she looked like her little sister. Sandy's mom sat up in bed and asked her if she had reported the rape. Sandy told her "no."

Her mom's next question was, "Where is the baby?"

Sandy told her mom that she was giving her up for adoption. Her mom asked her what she really wanted to do. Sandy was not sure of anything. Sandy just wanted something, but she did not know what that was. Sandy didn't know how to ask for it. Sandy was in a daze and she didn't know how to get out of it. Sandy needed help, and she was hoping she could get it from her family. Sandy's mom had Sandy call the welfare office to let them know that they wanted to come and pick up the baby the next day. Sandy's mom called the family friend Sandy had called the same week she wanted to go home after the rape happened. The three of them went to pick up a baby Sandy did not want. Sandy had to do everything she could to keep herself from running and screaming down the street. Sandy didn't want her, yet part of her felt she had to do this. She had to take care of this child. She had to do the right thing. Sandy was expected to do the right thing. Sandy needed to be punished for her failure. This was her punishment for what she let happen. Sandy had to carry that shame and guilt around with her forever. Sandy had done something wrong. Sandy had to face the punishment. The punishment was caring for the baby.

They got home late that afternoon. Everyone was excited about the baby. Sandy wasn't excited. Sandy just wanted to run and hide. Sandy put on an act, letting everyone believe she was happy. Inside, Sandy was dying. Sandy's mom took care of the baby girl most of that day and night. Sandy did as much as she could. Sandy didn't sleep at all that night. Sandy tried holding her. Sandy felt nothing for her. Sandy couldn't feel anything for her. Sandy already failed her. The sun was rising and Sandy's mom was getting out of bed. Sandy was sitting in the living room with the baby in her arms, trying to be happy with what was happening. Sandy didn't know what was going to happen over the next several days.

All she could think about was getting out. Sandy just wanted to run away and never come back.

Chapter 5

Over the next several days Sandy had several things she had to do before school started. Sandy had to put the babies' name on the birth certificate, find a place to live off campus, find a babysitter, and shop for baby things and household items.

The first thing was to give the baby a name; Sandy named her Nikki after a friend she played basketball with. Sandy's sister gave her a middle name of Amy. Sandy went to the hospital record office to add the name to the birth certificate. She found a studio apartment, and a daycare to watch the baby while she went to classes, she bought clothes, and household items needed to take care of the baby. She went home and Sandy's mom showed her how to bathe the baby, change diapers, feeding her and what to do when she cried.

On Friday Sandy and her mom went to the school housing office to find out what Sandy needed to do to let the school know she was not going to be living on campus next semester. Sandy was told by the housing director that all new students had to live on campus. Sandy explained to her. Sandy could not live on campus with a baby. The housing director appeared to be stunned. She thought Sandy was giving the baby up for adoption.

It was Saturday, and students were starting to arrive back at school. They went to Sandy dorm room. They got her things from there and took them to her new apartment. Sandy didn't like being in the apartment. Sandy didn't want to be at the dorm picking up her things. By having to leave the dorm it was as if it was being thrown back into her face. How bad a person she was to have let this happen. How were people going to look at her, what are people going to think of her and what was she going to do? Sandy knew nothing about babies; she could barely take care of herself, let alone a baby. Sandy had proven that to herself already because if she could take care of herself she would never have been raped. Sandy would never have had a child. Sandy would never be where she was at that moment. Classes started that week. Sandy began going back to school; she spent eight to ten hours a day at school, studying, training for the upcoming track season, or working in the athletic training room, trying to forget the life she had away from school. Sandy tried to forget the responsibilities of having a child.

The first week was the hardest. Sandy had this child to take care of and nobody around to help. Sandy looked at the baby and became angry about the situation she was in. The baby's crying made it worse. By Friday Sandy was going crazy. Sandy called home. She told her mom she couldn't do this. Sandy's mom came and picked up the baby and left her sister behind. Sandy told her sister she wanted to drink. Sandy's sister told her that was why mom wanted her to stay with her. Her sister was there that weekend to take care of her and keep her from drinking. It didn't matter if her sister was there or not, Sandy didn't have any money to buy any alcohol. Sandy had used all her money for the apartment, phone, utilities, food, and baby things. So unless she went to a bar and someone bought her drinks, she wasn't drinking that weekend. Her sister was too young for the bar and she didn't want to drink and drive. Sandy apartment was too far away from the bars to walk.

Sandy felt so alienated from everyone. Sandy knew things were going to change. Sandy didn't realize how much at the time. Sandy could barely accept what was going on, let alone deal with what was happening. Sandy pushed everything else aside. Sandy cut herself off from everyone around her. Sandy walked around most of the time in a fog. The only time she was able to deal with anything was during class times. She was able to focus on her classes. Sandy enjoyed being in classes and away for everything else. Sandy spent as much time as possible doing school work. Sandy hated going home every night. Sandy knew what was waiting for her when she got home. As soon as she picked up the baby from the sitter, the shame and guilt came over her. While she was in classes, she was just like every other student in school. Sandy wasn't different so she didn't have to feel the guilt and shame. Sunday had come and the baby was back and her sister was gone. Going to classes the next day seemed harder. Sandy didn't want to go to classes that day. She wanted to stay home alone.

Sandy knew that if she spent every second of the day caring for a baby she didn't want, she probably would have lost her mind. As a new parent, single, and trying to find out what she was going to do. That time was so difficult for Sandy. How was she going to make this all work, not knowing what was going to happen to them.

Chapter 6

Sandy went to therapy once a week. The first couple of months she didn't have much to say. Sandy was not sure what she was supposed to do in therapy. Then she realized that she would not be running track this season or any other season. Sandy no longer was able to play basketball either. Sandy lost it. Things in her life that made her happy were taken away. She was not allowed to do what she wanted. Sandy now had new responsibilities and obligations. This even made it harder to get past. Sandy failed again, because she was not living the life she wanted. Sandy had to live the life everyone else expected of her.

Sandy did not know how to find a way to fit this child into her life. Should she leave this child behind? The confusion she felt with the responsibility of keeping the child and the responsibility she felt she had to her family to keep the child she knew was not the baby's fault. She did not ask to come into this world. Sandy had to decide what to do. Sandy had to stick it out no matter what.

Sandy called a social worker to find out her options. The social worker came over to Sandy's apartment and told her that the child could be placed in foster care until she decided on what she wanted to do. Put the child in foster care until Sandy was able to keep her or put her up for adoption, like she had planned. Sandy couldn't let her go with the social worker. Sandy felt that if she let her go, that was one more failure. She didn't want to be a failure anymore. Failing at getting away from her attacker was one thing, but failing this child was totally different. *What would she think of me?* Sandy thought. What was she to do? How could she do this and keep her own life?

Sandy started drinking beer at night when she got home from classes. Then the drinking became even more frequent. She wanted to drink in the morning when she woke up. By the time she got to her first class, she was ready for another. Sandy started drinking all the time. When she woke in the morning, she grabbed a pitcher and filled it with ice, then vodka and then orange juice. Her first drink of the day was a screwdriver. She would put the pitcher in the car. It was winter time and it stayed cold. Sandy put her daughter in her car seat and then would driver her to daycare. Then Sandy went to school, she parked as close as she could to her classroom. Sandy filled up her mug right before her first class. Sandy went to her car in between classes if she had time and filled it up again. By the time noon came around most days Sandy had about four glasses. At lunch she sat in her car and drank. If Sandy was meeting friends or eating on campus in one of the cafeterias she left the cup in the car. Usually by the time she had to be in the training room at 2:30 p.m., as part of her degree. Sandy had about eight drinks during the day. Nobody seemed to notice that she had been drinking. Nobody ever said anything to her about being drunk. Sandy made sure that she had breath mints, gum, and snacks with her all the time. Most people couldn't tell that she had been drinking. Just to be on the safe side before she would go to the training room, she grabbed a can of pop. Sandy hid her drinking very well. Anybody who knew her did not know she drank. When she was out with friends, she didn't drink. It was when she felt alone that she drank. Sandy felt most alone during classes, at home, and when she was driving in the car. Even if Nikki was there, Sandy was drinking. She didn't care. All she wanted to do was die. Even if it was a slow death, Even if it meant dying in a car crash. Sandy drank for about a year and a half. The days were all the same. She went through the motion of living. If she was going to her parents for the weekend, she didn't drink, but if she was alone at home or if she was with Nikki at home she spent most of the day drinking.

Sandy began opening up more in therapy. Sandy began asking questions as to why? Sandy went and talked about anything and every thing; she talked about the rape and the baby. Sometimes Sandy talked about how she was feeling and how she was dealing with everything. After about eight months into therapy, Sandy started to speak to old friends. Sandy even started seeing an ex-boyfriend. He came over once and a while and helped her with different things. He talked about things that were happening in his life with his family. They started to become really close again after a few months. Sandy began to feel comfortable and the fear, shame, and feelings of failure started to go away when he was around. The safety she used to feel was coming back. At this time she was not ready for any type of relationship. He understood and did not push the issue of dating and intimacy. They were friends, and he gave her the support she needed. Sandy's drinking stayed about the same. Even going to therapy didn't help with the drinking. Usually after therapy she wanted to drink even more. Some of the therapy sessions were very difficult to deal with. Drinking helped her to cut off her feelings because she didn't like how she felt. It gave her a way to escape the pain and the nightmare she was living.

Spring break was coming up. Her parents bought her a plane ticket to go see her gram, so Gram could meet her first great-grandchild. At the time, Sandy thought it was a good idea. She needed to get away.

The day came for Nikki and her to leave. Sandy was excited. Then things changed. As they arrived at the airport, Sandy's aunt and uncle picked them up. When Sandy saw them across the terminal, this over whelming fear came over her. She looked at them and they looked back at her. The shame, guilt, and feeling of failure swept over Sandy. The way she perceived them looking at her brought back those feelings. Sandy became very nervous. Sandy believed she knew what they were thinking, but she didn't know what they were told. Sandy knew she didn't call and tell them she was raped and kept a child she didn't want. She didn't know if her mom had told them anything, either. As Sandy walked toward them, she put on a happy face, pushing all the feelings she was having aside. Sandy gave them each a hug. They seemed happy to see her and the baby. Sandy's uncle helped her get the luggage as her aunt watched

Nikki. They all got into the car and headed to Gram's house.

They arrived at Gram's house, and Gram was waiting at the front door holding it open. Sandy got to the door first with Nikki. She gave them a hug. They walked in the house, and Sandy gave Nikki to Gram. Sandy went back outside to help with the luggage. By the time Sandy got to the bottom of the steps, her aunt and uncle got everything and were on their way into the house. Sandy held open the door. She sat on the couch as they took turns holding Nikki.

That week spent with them was long and hard. Every day someone new would come over to see Nikki. Aunts, uncles, and cousins all came over. Even some great aunts came over. It seemed that every time Sandy turned around someone new was there.

When no one was there, Sandy was okay. The emotions would dissipate. Every time someone came over all those feelings would come rushing back. At night when everyone was as sleep, was when Sandy had the most peace. Every morning Sandy would have to get the nerve to come out of the bedroom. Nikki wanting to be feed each morning helped her get up and out of the room. Nikki enjoyed all the attention. Nikki was a very happy baby, while all Sandy could do was *act* happy.

Sandy was glad when it was time to go home. The day they were to leave, Sandy made sure they were packed and ready to go. Sandy made sure she had plenty of bottles for Nikki. Her aunt and uncle came to pick them up to go to the airport. They got on the plane and Sandy was so glad when she and Nikki got home.

It was one thing hiding everything from her family. But having to hide it from the extended family was even more difficult. Sandy thought that was because she had no place to hide while she was there. Back home, she had her own apartment. Sandy could hide all she wanted.

Chapter 7

Sandy's therapist gave her some suggestions on how to deal with her feelings. She had Sandy start a journal. Writing down what she was feeling. Her therapist told her she could put anything she wanted into the journal. Keeping a journal is not just about words and she told Sandy that she could use pictures to show her emotions. Her therapist wanted Sandy to express what she was feeling at a specific moment time. Sandy wrote about how she wanted to feel. Sandy wrote two to three times a week. Every time she sat down to write in the journal, Sandy drank even more. The only way Sandy could let out the feelings was with a drink. It seemed to be easier to write when she had been drinking. Sandy was able to let go of what she was feeling. She used drinking to feel. Even if the feelings only lasted for a short time. She was able to feel something.

The problem with getting in touch with your feeling while being drunk is the feelings are not always real and she never really was able to deal with them. The feelings only lasted as long as she was drunk. Sandy stopped feeling when she passed out for the evening.

After a year of drinking and a year of being in therapy, Sandy's therapist found out about her drinking. During a session, Sandy became frustrated. Sandy had several things go wrong that day. Nikki had a doctor's appointment. The doctor was running behind. That made her late for her therapy appointment. She had to drop Nikki off at the sitters. On the way to dropping Nikki off Sandy was pulled over for speeding. Since Sandy was already late, she stopped at the store to buy a twelve-pack of beer. Sandy opened a can and poured it into the fast food cup she kept in the car. She had three drinks on her way to the therapy appointment. Sandy was angry and frustrated. That past week was really horrible. It seemed everything was going wrong. By the time she reached the therapist's office Sandy was about fifteen minutes late and feeling the effects of the alcohol. The therapist noticed Sandy had been drinking. She asked Sandy how much she had to drink. Sandy told her a lie. She told her that she only had a couple of drinks. The truth was that she had about five or six drinks that day. She asked Sandy how often she was drinking. Sandy told her another lie. She told her that she only drank once and a while. The therapist didn't believe what Sandy was telling her. The therapist knew Sandy was drinking more than she said. The therapist asked Sandy when she had her last drink today. Sandy told her it was right before her appointment, before she had left the house. This was another lie Sandy told. It was in the car on the way to see the therapist. It was sitting out in her car waiting for her when the appointment was over. The therapist kept pushing, trying to find out the true amount she was drinking. By the end of the session the therapist knew Sandy drank daily and spent most of the evenings drinking. The therapist told Sandy that if she did not stop drinking she would have Nikki taken away. She told Sandy she had two weeks to get help with her drinking problem.

Sandy went home that evening and thought about what the therapist had said as she finished drinking the last of the beer she had bought earlier. If they took Nikki away because she was drinking, then she would have failed as a parent. Sandy didn't want to be a failure any longer. Sandy wanted to stop failing at everything she did. What was she going to do? She thought to herself. If she stopped drinking then she would stop feeling. Sandy shut down everything. No emotions allowed. She could not allow herself to have any emotions. Sandy built a wall to protect herself from the emotions. She took the feelings she had and buried them. If Sandy stayed within the walls and kept the emotions buried, she believed that she couldn't get hurt, she couldn't fail and she could make it through another day.

The problems with building a wall and burying the emotions is that nothing gets through the wall and then you don't have to deal with what you are feeling.

Sandy finally made her decision after about a week. Sandy was going to stop drinking. She changed her daily routine. She stopped drinking. She woke up that morning and instead of fixing herself a drink she made a cup of tea. No matter how much Sandy wanted a drink she did not allow herself to have one. It was difficult for the first two months. Sandy had to fight the urge to drink.

The urge to drink was so strong at times, but Sandy was too ashamed to go to anyone for help. Sandy believed that by asking and admitting she needed help with a drinking problem she had failed again. Sandy wanted to drink, but she kept telling herself that Nikki would be taken away if she did. So that fear of failure stopped her from drinking. Sandy was more afraid of failure than anything else.

Sandy had to find something to keep herself from drinking. That spring she bought a used bike and an infant carrier. After classes, Sandy would pick up Nikki and get ready to go for a ride. They spent an hour or two each night riding around town. Sandy was finally able to release some of the stress she was feeling. It felt good exercising again. By the time summer had come they were able to ride three or four hours a day.

That summer, Sandy took two classes the first session to help keep her active. She was afraid if she didn't keep doing something then she might go back to drinking.

Starting to ride the bike gave her a release to deal with some of the emotions she was unable to bury. Sandy had not had a way to release her feelings for a very long time. After Nikki was born, Sandy took her home. She had stopped running. She felt that she had lost everything. So she started to give up everything. Sandy couldn't take her running with her and she couldn't leave her home alone. Now she was older and able to do more things. Sandy could fit everything in a backpack. Most of the time Nikki would fall asleep in her seat and didn't wake up until they arrived back home. Sandy was feeling like her sanity was returning. She seemed to be happier. She felt as if things were getting better. It felt like she was getting better. She didn't worry about failing as much. She seemed to finally enjoying having Nikki in her life. Sandy was starting to allow herself to care about the child she never wanted.

Chapter 8

After about a year and a half, Sandy stopped going to therapy. Sandy knew she was better and no longer needed any more therapy.

Sandy went to the college housing administrator asked if she could tell her story to the resident assistance. The meeting was set up for a weekday evening. They sat in a big circle. Everyone was looking at Sandy. It was difficult. Sandy couldn't look at anyone's face. She started to tell them what happened. Sandy started to cry and stopped talking to hold back the tears. She stared at the floor. Sandy started talking again about what happened, telling them as much as she could remember as to what happened that night. Sandy answered questions from people after she was done. She answered them the best she could. How she felt and what she was feeling at that moment was difficult to talk about and deal with. Sandy didn't know much about feelings other than anger, failure, disappointment, shame, and maybe a few others. By telling these people her story, Sandy hoped that those feelings would go away. Maybe if they didn't look at her differently then maybe other people were not looking at her differently either. Sandy believed by telling them, maybe somehow she could get rid of those feelings. Even though she told them her story the feelings did not go away. Sandy still felt that people looked at her differently.

Sandy began taking more psychology classes. The psychology classes were teaching her stages of development and parenting. It taught her what she needed to give to this child, and to better understand what this child needed from her.

Then it happened again. Sandy felt like she was losing control. It was becoming hard to go to classes every day. It was hard at times to just get up in the morning. She wanted to run away. She wanted to find some place that she could go where no one would ever find her.

Sandy started therapy again. The therapist she had before had moved her practice. Sandy had to start over with a new therapist. Sandy had to start to trust someone new. It took several weeks before she was able to talk about what was happening to her; why she felt she had to run and why she was constantly praying that she would disappear forever. She was looking for something to help her run away. Sandy found that by drinking she could run from everything that was going on. Sandy knew she could not go back there. She needed to find some other way to run and hide. She needed to find something that would give her a way to escape even if for a little while.

Sandy found a way to deal with everything. Her friend

was still around. She decided that it was time to move forward. He came over Friday night. Nikki was at her grandparents for the weekend. That night she forced herself to have sex with him. There were parts she enjoyed and others that brought back some of the horrible memories and emotions of that night. Sandy did what she always did, she buried those feelings. Over the next several months they became close, he was very gentle and he took his time when they had sex. He was patient and if she needed to stop or could not go any further, he stopped. Many times Sandy did not have to tell him how she was feeling, many times he knew. As time went on, Sandy became bolder. Anytime he came over, that was all she wanted. She didn't care about him or anything else. She just wanted to feel something that gave her a little bit of pleasure and let her escape from everything going on around her. Sandy just wanted to feel something. This went on for about a year.

Sandy found that she was pregnant again. Sandy did not want this child. She told him she was pregnant, and that she had to have an abortion because of medical reasons. That was not the truth. Sandy could have other children. Granted, there was a chance of complications as with the first, but she was young and healthy. Sandy made an appointment with an abortion clinic. They drove to the clinic for the appointment. They sat in the waiting room for what seemed like forever. After a while they were taken into a room and a counselor came in. The nurse talked to them about what was going to happen and she asked them questions. Making sure they knew what they were doing. Sandy knew what she had to do.

There was no way anyone was going to keep her from doing what she knew was right. After they were done talking, she was taken into another room. There, she was given a gown. Sandy changed into the gown and sat on the exam table waiting for the doctor to come in. The doctor came in to give an exam, making sure that she was not too far along. He left and the nurse started an IV. The nurse left and again Sandy sat alone in the room. Sitting in that room alone, Sandy started to question her decision. She knew it was the best thing for her to do. Having another child was not something she wanted. The doctor came in and she was taken into a surgical room to start the abortion. Sandy laid on the table with her arm over her eyes, holding back the tears. As the doctor began the abortion it became harder to hold the tears back. The pain from the abortion increased the longer it went on. Once it was over, Sandy was taken to a recovery room and her friend was brought back to sit with her. Sandy made sure the tears were gone and made sure that when he saw her she was as confident as when she went in. A few hours later they left. They went and picked up Nikki and went home. He stayed while she slept. When she woke up, she made dinner and he left.

After she had the abortion, their relationship grew very strained. He wanted children. Sandy did not. Sandy already had a child that she never wanted. Why bring another child into this world?

That evening, Sandy felt the emotional pain from the abortion; she called her therapist. The therapist opened her office and Sandy went to see her. Sandy told her what she had done, and she began to cry. She told her that she had to grieve over the loss of this child. Part of her did want this child even though a greater part did not. The pain Sandy was feeling was normal and she needed to come to grips with her emotions and the decision she had made. Sandy realized that there were two very strong reasons that she did not want this child. The first being she did not want to disappointment her parent. Her parents didn't believe her about the rape. They never said it out right to Sandy that they didn't believe her, but Sandy knew they didn't. Sandy got the feeling by the comments that where made. Second, how could she love one child more than the other? She couldn't see them as being the same. Love them the same, and care about them the same. One came from something horrible, the other out of some type of need or desperation Sandy realized at that point having other children was not something she wanted. Sandy took the steps to make sure that the chances of her ever getting pregnant again were as small as possible.

About a month after the abortion, her friend stopped coming around. He stopped calling. Sandy decided to move on. She had to have sex. She craved the feeling and desire that came from sex. When Nikki was with her parents or sometimes if she could find someone to watch her, she spent her nights at the bar. Sandy did what she could to attract a man. When she found someone to have sex with, she had to decide where they were going to end up. If Nikki was with her parents, Sandy sometimes brought them home with her. If Sandy had a babysitter, Sandy had to go to their place. When the sex was over, she left. Sandy didn't want it to become emotional. Sandy didn't allow herself to have emotions during sex. Sandy didn't want sex to mean anything. She needed sex. Sex was just like the alcohol, she needed it to feel something. It was a way for her to get the high she so desperately craved. It was a way for her to feel something other than the guilt and shame that she felt the rest of the time.

The desire of feeling the physical was stronger than anything else. Sandy had a need to be close to someone, even if it was for a short time. Sandy started taking birth control pills. When she first started having sex, she didn't use condoms. The idea of getting a sexually transmitted disease such as AIDS or HIV, at first, didn't matter. After a while, this feeling of guilt came over her. If she got AIDS or HIV and she died then she had failed again. To stop the feelings of guilt and failure she started to use condoms. Part of her didn't care if she died of a sexually transmitted disease. Most of those early days all Sandy wanted to do was die. Sandy spent the next two years meeting guys, going out, having sex. If the sex was good, she kept them around for a few months. When she felt that they wanted more, she moved onto the next person. Most of the time, they were just one-night stands.

Sandy's first one-night stand was the worst. Somehow knowing that she was just having sex for the sake of having sex was difficult for her. Sandy grew up believing that having sex with someone was something that was supposed to be special. That having sex and being in love was the same thing. After the night of the rape, sex no longer had a connection with loving someone. Sex was something to make her feel good. So that first one-night stand was difficult. In some way she still believed they were connected. When the sex was over, she left. When Sandy got home, she felt this ache inside. Sandy did what she always did, she pushed the feeling aside. After a while, having sex became easier. The aching feeling disappeared.

All Sandy wanted was physical pleasure. She didn't want any commitments or relationships. Sometimes the person she had sex with did not understand that was all she wanted. They wanted to keep coming back and hang around. Sandy had a need to be close to someone, even if for a short time. Sandy needed to know that, sexually, she was okay. Sandy needed to be desired. Sandy needed to feel the physical pleasure of sex without having any emotional tie to someone. The emotions were the thing she did not want. If emotions were tied to the physical pleasure, then somehow in her mind she really did like being raped. Sandy wanted what had happened to happen. Sandy believed that she enjoyed what he did to her. By having sex and no emotional tie, it let her know that no matter how her body reacted, it didn't mean she liked what happened that night. It didn't mean she wanted it to happen. Still, to this day, she did not fully understand why this need was so important. She still now, at times, craved the pleasure she got from sex. Sandy could control the need for having sex. When she got that craving she could let the emotions in and enjoy them. There were still times that having sex just for the physical pleasure was important to her. It didn't happen as often as it did before. Sandy got a little better each time she had sex.

Sandy did have male friends. They brought her down from the need or desire she craved so deeply. They helped with some of the stability she so desperately needed. Sandy did think about having sex with them. She was able to control those desires. Sandy wanted friends.

She felt she needed friends. Some of them new she was raped, but others did not and she was not going to tell them.

Only a select few knew Sandy's horrible secret. They treated her with kindness and gave her what she needed from their friendship. Part of Sandy thought that if she had sex with these friends that maybe they wouldn't believe her. Another part knew that by not having sex with them she could let them into her life. Sandy was able to share things with them. She could sometimes let go of what she was feeling. Sandy could not let the emotion and the sex interact with each other. Sandy had to keep the emotions buried when having sex. If she started to feel emotions when having sex with someone she knew it was time to move onto the next person. Sandy believed that if the two interacted, she would lose control of everything, that everything she had worked so hard for would be gone. Sandy wouldn't be able to handle the emotions and sex together.

Sandy never let the one-night stands know about the rape. Sandy didn't care what they thought about her. She was just using them, anyway, but her male friends, she needed them to believe in her. Sandy was grateful for the male friends she had back then. She felt lucky they came into her life at that time. Sandy needed their friendship. She needed them to believe in her.

Chapter 9

Sandy's life with her daughter, Nikki ,through those years of college was the hardest. Sandy had grown to love her in her own way after the first six months of her life. Nikki was the strength she needed sometimes to make it through another day. During the first few years of Nikki's life she spent a lot of time in daycare, or with Sandy's family. Nikki went to Sandy's parent's house on the weekends, and stayed until Sunday or Monday when Sandy's mom brought her back. Sandy spent some weekends at her parent's house, but most of the time she stayed in their apartment at school. Sandy gave everything she could to Nikki, but Nikki gave Sandy so much more.

When Nikki was two years old she started potty training. Sandy found out that Nikki had a medical condition that caused her to be in the hospital for several days at a time. She got very sick. Sandy wondered why this was happening to her. Sandy did her part; this child was going to be sick all her life. Part of Sandy had feelings for this child, another part of her felt as if she had a duty to this child. Sandy didn't like the emotional part she felt for her. Emotions were not something Sandy could deal with. Sandy didn't like emotions. They were always better off buried than on the surface. Somehow Sandy could let emotions show when it came to Nikki. Sandy let many emotions show, as long as she could control the emotions and let only the emotions she wanted out. Sandy knew that she was never really her child. Sandy saw her as if she was a person she had to help grow into an adult. Sandy was only there to teach her right from wrong and make sure she was safe and protected without failing, always hoping she was not failing her.

Sandy had to find a way to deal with her being sick. Sandy had to be the one to make sure that she got all the medical treatment she needed to try and fix Nikki's medical problem. Nikki was born with a small left kidney that functioned only 20% of the time. Her right kidney functioned at 80%. She got urinary tract infections that turned into blood stream infections. That put Nikki in the hospital for weeks at a time. Nikki saw one specialist after another for the next three years. When she was in the hospital, Sandy stayed day and night, only sleeping a few hours. Sandy only left Nikki if her mom was there. Sandy left long enough to go home and shower. Then Sandy would return to her side. At times, Sandy thought if she died, then her punishment would be over, but if she died then Sandy would have failed again. Sandy failed to keep her safe. Sandy failed to protect her. Nikki had to survive so Sandy would not fail.

The fear of failure was stronger than the desire for the punishment to end. Sandy needed to be punished for what happened. Sandy had to punish herself for what happened. Sandy had to because there was no one else to punish or blame but herself.

By the time Nikki was 5, the potty training was over. It was rough getting through those years Sandy knew mentally she could not help herself, but emotionally she wanted this stage of her life to be over. Sandy did not want to deal with the doctors, the medical treatments, and everything that went along with it. It put even more of a drain on her emotionally; Sandy was having a hard time trying to care and bring herself to love this person, let alone have to deal with the medical issues.

Sandy wanted her to know that she did what she could to protect her. Sandy wanted to protect her, because she did not get protected. Sandy was raped; nobody was around to protect her. Sandy was all alone that night and for the most part Sandy still felt alone most of the time. Nobody was there to protect her after the rape happened. Sandy felt as if she had no one and she could never let Nikki feel that nobody cared about her. Sandy shared what emotions she allowed herself to feel. Sandy often wondered if she gave Nikki enough.

Now that Nikki is a young adult, Sandy wonders if she failed her.

Chapter 10

After Sandy graduated from college, she moved back home for a few months, and then moved out west. Sandy wanted to go to out west and go to graduate school, but instead ended up out west and stayed with her gram for about nine months. Sandy worked two jobs; one at a gas station at night, the other at a restaurant during the evening. Preschool started for Nikki and Sandy tried to sleep while Nikki was in school. When Sandy got home she would take Nikki to school in the morning and pick her up at noon. When Sandy had time off from work, she went to the school and volunteered.

After several months of being there, Sandy started dating. Sandy went out with a guy for several months. It was actually dating. Sandy didn't go out with him for just sexual satisfaction and she went out with him to get more of the emotional pieces she was missing. They dated for several months and they had fun, he did not have a problem letting Nikki come along when they did things. He actually enjoyed spending time with Nikki and playing with her. Sandy hadn't seen a therapist in more than two years. Sandy felt she was better. Sandy had moved on and things were as good as they were going to get. Then one night working at the gas station during the graveyard shift, the store was robbed. The man came in, looked around the store, came to the register and asked if that was her car outside. Sandy answered him with a "yes." Sandy turned to go look at the car, thinking maybe someone was messing with her car. He asked her for the keys. Sandy looked at him told him she was not giving him the keys; he pulled out a gun, and told her to give him the money in the register. Sandy opened up the register and gave him the money, and then he asked for the car keys again. Sandy didn't want to give up her car, but she did. She handed him the keys and he walked out, she picked up the phone and called the police. The police came and took a report. A few hours later they caught the man with her car and the money. He was put in jail. He wrecked Sandy's car. The transmission was gone. The car was taken into evidence, and she was given a ride back to work. Sandy worked several days as if nothing had happened. She had to rely on other people to get Nikki to school now since she did not have a car. The person she was dating picked her up in the morning, took her home and took Nikki to school. At noon she walked to pick her up.

After a few weeks of fighting with the insurance company, they paid for her car. She was able to buy a used piece of junk to get her where she needed to go. When fighting with the insurance company, dealing with police and court hearings the stress was gone. It happened, the nightmares began, the fears came up, and

Sandy started losing control of everything around her. Sandy's employer gave her the option of going to a doctor for medication or to therapy. Sandy went to therapy again. Just what she needed was to start therapy all over again. Maybe this wouldn't be so bad since it was just a robbery. It had nothing to do with anything else. Little did Sandy know that everything that happens in life is somehow connected. Sandy's mind had a new opportunity to bring up everything from the past.

Sandy started to go to therapy once a week. It came time for her first appointment. The therapist spent the session asking about her background, family, friends, and experiences. They were simple questions to answer. The next session she asked Sandy about the robbery. She wanted to know what happened that night. What it felt like when it happened, what she had experience. Sandy could not explain her experience or what she felt. Sandy had no clue what emotions she had experienced. Sandy had no idea what emotions were. Sandy knew anger, frustration, and fear. Sandy had those feelings before with the rape. Sandy knew how mad she was at herself, she was frustrated by her failure, and she was afraid it happened again. But the robbery, Sandy could not figure out. The therapist asked Sandy to describe what happened, what she saw, and what she remembered about that night. Sandy described what happened step-by-step. Sandy described the man from the time he walked into the store. The therapist stopped her and asked her how it made her feel. It was just a person walking in a building. Sandy didn't know that she really felt anything. He walked around the store, he seemed to be searching for something. How did she feel, the therapist asked. Sandy had no clue as to how she felt. Sandy didn't know that she was supposed to feel something by people passing through her life. Sandy could not answer her questions. Sandy was becoming frustrated. Sandy told her that she felt that the questions the therapist was asking were stupid! Sandy did not know what this had to do with the nightmares, depression, fear, and anxiety she was feeling now. The next week the therapist let her talk about what had happened the past week and what she did. Sandy let her know about the nightmares, and what would happen in each nightmare. One of Sandy's most vivid nightmares, and the one she still remembers, was:

She is in a cabin in the woods, with friends and family members. It is nighttime; she hears a noise outside of the cabin. Nobody else seems to hear it. A rock is thrown through the window. An axe chopping down the door, nobody else sees what she sees. They are all laughing and having fun and a man with no face comes in and starts pulling her out of the cabin by her feet. She can't scream, she can't run away and nobody will help her get away for the man without a face. She grabs hold of the furniture in the room to try and keep him from pulling her out of the cabin. When he gets her out of the cabin, he beats her and the dream ends.

The therapist asked how the dream made her feel. Sandy was terrified as to what was going to happen to her. She was angry that her family and friends did not help her. Sandy was afraid she'd be raped. The therapist asked why rape came to mind. Sandy was robbed at a gunpoint as far as the therapist knew. The therapist asked if anything else happen that night of the robbery. Did he touch her? did he make any type of sexual advance? Sandy told her that he just asked for money and her car. The therapist asked about the rape in Sandy's dream and why the rape came up. Sandy told her that she was raped in college. This dumbfounded look came over the therapist's face. The therapist asked if Sandy went to counseling or ever talked about the rape. Sandy told her about the therapy she had before. The therapist explained to Sandy that the trauma of the robbery brought back the emotions of the rape. The therapist sent Sandy to a psychiatrist for medications and medical evaluation. Sandy was diagnosed with post-traumatic stress disorder. What is post-traumatic stress disorder? Sandy was blown away that she could have this and not even know about it. It was explained that the trauma from the robbery had stirred up the trauma from the rape. Sandy thought she had worked past the trauma from the rape. So the therapy continued. This time the therapist tried to bring out Sandy's feelings. After about three months of therapy, Sandy decided that it was time to move on.

Sandy packed her bags and moved again. This time Nikki and Sandy moved with the guy she was dating. They packed up and moved to the state capital. By that time, the relationship was over, Sandy had determined that they were better off just being friends. The romantic part of the relationship died shortly after the robbery. Like most of Sandy's romantic relationships, if it lasted more than six months that meant that they were getting to close and she had to bail. But he did not want to give up on the relationship. Sandy told him the only way he was moving with her and Nikki was as a roommate. Sandy was done with the relationship. He accepted that he was just a friend and roommate. It became difficult having a relationship that meant she had to rely on someone. No one could be there for her. So before things went any further, Sandy ended the emotional part of the relationship. Sandy hated to ask for help from people. Sandy had this need and desire to do everything on her own, in her own way with her own agenda. Sandy did not want help because it messed everything up. If Sandy couldn't do it by herself, then she didn't need to do it at all. Sandy did not want to rely on anybody for help, especially a man. Sandy was hoping to go back to school, she was not using the degree she spent so much time earning. Sandy thought that maybe if she went back to school and got a master's degree she would be able to find better employment. When they moved, they had no place to live. They put all there stuff in a storage locker. It was the beginning of summer. So they lived in campgrounds for about a month as they searched the newspaper and drove around neighborhoods to see what they could find. Finally, they found a three-bedroom house. Little did Sandy know she should have kept on looking for a place. It seemed like a nice neighborhood, but in fact it was not. They lived there for nine month and were robbed five times in the last three months they lived there. They had TVs, VCRs, money, and other things come up missing. They had one break-in where they damaged the walls in one of the bedrooms. They punched holes in the wall going from one bedroom to the other. Sandy called her landlord told them that she was moving out. They fixed up the rooms as best they could. He worked days and Sandy worked nights, so she did not have to pay for daycare. He found a mobile home; Sandy filled out an application to buy the trailer from the owner. They moved into the trailer about three weeks later. They lived there about eight months. Nikki loved the school she was in. Sandy had finally found a job within her field of study and everything seemed to be working out.

Then they received a notice on the door that the true owner of the trailer was evicting them. The couple Sandy was making payments to did not make their payments to the actual person who owned the trailer. Just when she thought things were going good, Sandy got slapped in the face again. Sandy had to hire an attorney. She had to take time off work to go to court, and finally after two months, the matter was settled. She had to make payments to the true owner. He had been convicted of bad real estate deals previously. Sandy made sure that every payment was made on time. She had invested too much time and money into the trailer already and she was not about to give it up without a fight. Sandy filed a lawsuit against the couple who sold her the trailer to get part of her money back. Sandy started working two jobs to make sure that she had enough money to make the payments each month. It had been almost two years since the robbery.

Out of the blue, the workers' compensation insurance company wanted to make a settlement for the robbery. Sandy was amazed that they wanted to give her money for the robbery. The insurance company set up an appointment for her to go see a psychiatrist for psychological testing. Sandy agreed to go to the appointment. Thinking that it would be easy taking the test they wanted her to take. About two weeks after her appointment the insurance company contacted her and offered her a settlement. Sandy agreed to the amount they offered. It was enough to pay off the trailer and some other bills.

Sandy was feeling good. Finally everything in her life was going the way she wanted. Sandy had a nice home for Nikki, she was at a good school, and she had the job she always wanted. Money was not so hard to come by. Bills were paid on time. Sandy did not have to worry about money to pay the bills or for food. After about six months Sandy was able to save up enough money for a down payment to buy a new car. Sandy's sister was getting married and she needed some transportation to get her and Nikki 1200 miles to the wedding. It was way too expensive to fly. Sandy didn't like to fly anyway. Things seem to be going great. Sandy felt like finally her life is working out. Sandy was hoping that she could buy a house in a few years.

Chapter 11

Sandy luck continued. She had won a lottery jackpot in the amount of $20,000.00. Sandy couldn't believe that she had won. Sandy had gone down to the corner store to purchase her tickets for that evening. She didn't have enough cash with her. Sandy had some old tickets that she had not checked in the car. Sandy was hoping that she had won enough money to by her tickets for the next week. The man behind the counter ran the tickets through the computer. He stated that he was unable to cash one of the tickets, but he could cash the other one. Sandy purchased her tickets for the week. Sandy asked the man why he could not cash the ticket. He told Sandy she had won the jackpot and needed to take the ticket down to the lottery commission down town.

Sandy went home to tell her roommate that the corner store could not cash her ticket. He thought the man at the corner store could cash up to $500. He took the ticket and looked up the numbers on the internet. He checked the dates and found that it was true. Sandy had won the jackpot. Sandy couldn't believe it. Sandy was in shock. She had to keep looking at the printout of the numbers and compare them to the ticket. Finally, after the shock wore off, she made a few phone calls. The first was to her mom. She spread the word to the rest of the family. The second call was to her supervisor, letting her know that she was going to be late for work. Her supervisor asked why and Sandy told her that she had to take a winning ticket to lottery commission the next morning. She understood and wanted Sandy to stop by the office after she was finished.

Sandy arrived at the lottery office. She handed the ticket to the lady behind the counter. She put the ticket in the machine and handed Sandy some paperwork. Sandy sat down and completed the paperwork. When she was finished, she handed the paperwork back to the lady behind the counter. The lady told her that it will take a while for them to print the check. About twenty minutes later, the lady called Sandy back to the counter and handed her the check for $13,800. Sandy went to see her supervisor after she left the lottery office. They sat in the supervisor's office, talking about what Sandy was going to do with the money. Sandy wanted to take Nikki on a trip she'd never forget. The supervisor told Sandy to give her at least a week notice before she took her vacation. Sandy explained to her supervisor that the vacation would have to wait until school was out. It was three and a half months until Nikki was done with school for the year.

Sandy took part of the money and paid off her car and had enough for her mom, sister, brother-in-law and their two daughters to go with them on vacation. When June came, they were all ready for vacation. They bought new clothes. Sandy took two weeks vacation. Sandy wanted to spend one week at the parks and then come back to spend time with her gram. Nikki and Sandy left three days before everyone else. Unfortunately, due to bad weather, Nikki and Sandy had a layover in Houston. The storm made it difficult for the plane to land, causing them to miss their connecting flight. The next morning they waited for a flight, they had to fly on stand-by. They finally made a flight and arrived that afternoon. Sandy and Nikki checked into their hotel. They spent several hours resting by the pool. They went out to dinner that night. The next morning they got up early and did some sightseeing. The place Nikki enjoyed the most that day was a farm. Nikki milked a cow, and went on a hay ride. That evening when they got back to the hotel, they had dinner at a fast food restaurant and spent the evening in the pool. Sandy spent the evening sitting and watching Nikki play. The next morning they slept in. They had to go back to the airport to exchange the rental car and picked up the van and everyone else at the airport. Everyone arrived safely. They all loaded up the van and headed to the hotel. They checked into the hotel and spent three days and two nights at the park. Everything was paid for in advance. They even had park dollars to spend. It was the first year for a new part of the park to open. They spent three days shopping, exploring, eating, and the kids spent most of their time trying to get the autographs of the park characters. When the three days were done, they went to another hotel to rest and relax. The next day they went to a space museum and the beach.

They arrived at the space museum and there was way more to see than Sandy had expected. They looked around for a few hours and then headed to the beach. They spent most of the afternoon at the beach playing in the ocean. They saw a stingray that swam right by Nikki's leg. The kids collected seashells. It was getting late and everyone was getting hungry. They packed up everything and headed back to the hotel, stopping at a roadside vender to buy fruit. On the road back to the hotel Sandy told everyone that Nikki and her were going back to the space museum the next day and they could come along if they wanted to.

The next day Sandy, her mom, and Nikki got up early and went back to the space museum. They spent a good eight to ten hours looking at everything. While they were there, they saw a space shuttle land. They went back to the hotel and told the others how good of a day they had. They made dinner and sat and talked while the kids swam in the pool.

The next day they had to go back home. Nikki and Sandy back to their home and the rest went back to their homes. Nikki and Sandy arrived home late that evening. They got their bags and went to their car and headed down to see Gram. Sandy drove all night and arrived early the next morning. Sandy and Nikki stayed with gram for five days. Sandy and Nikki went back home the following Saturday so Sandy could get ready to go back to work on the following Monday.

Chapter 12

It happened again. Eighteen months later Sandy was rear-ended in an auto accident. Her life changed again. Sandy hurt her right arm and upper back. After a year of treatment she had surgery to try and fix a nerve problem in her right hand. Sandy had the surgery and was out of work for several months. The surgery did not work completely. Sandy lost most of the feeling in her right hand. The damage to the nerve had already been done. Sandy lost her job and went into a deep depression for about three months. Sandy's roommate had left. He got married and moved a couple of trailers down. Sandy spent most of her time in her room sleeping, depressed, angry, waiting for the men in the white suits to take her away. Sandy only had her part-time job to support the household. Sandy was lucky the car and trailer were paid off. The only bills were lot rent, utilities, and food. Sandy could not seem to do much of anything she had even taken a break from her part-time job. Sandy was collecting unemployment, and that covered the expenses of the house, but left very little for anything extra. Sandy didn't care anyway. She just wanted to give everything up. Sandy felt like a lost cause. She wanted it to be over. Nothing in her life was working out. She felt Nikki would be better off with someone other than her and she would be better off dead. Sandy had a power of attorney made up so that if anything happened to her, Nikki would be taken care of financially. Sandy had her best friend agree to make sure that, financially, things were taken care of and that Nikki would get to her grandparents so they could take care of her. It took Sandy three and a half months to come out of the depression enough to try and go back to work and start thinking about what she was going to do with the rest of her life. Sandy no longer had a career. Sandy could no longer do her job and she had a long way to go before retirement.

Sandy went back to working nights and decided to go to paralegal school. It was hard to get out of bed three times a week and go to work at 4:00 p.m. Most of the time Sandy just wanted everything to end. Sandy wanted all the bad stuff to stop happening to her. It was just another sign that she was not worthy of having anything good in her life. The powers above would do anything to keep her from making any type of life for herself. Sandy believed she would continue to be punished the rest of her life and she did not understand why. By May the depression was slowly becoming better. Sandy was back in school studying to be a paralegal. Sandy was in school all day, then working a few hours at night a couple days a week. Sandy found a new roommate to move in to help cover expenses since she was back in school. It was hard for Sandy to get into changing careers. Sandy was very angry about giving up a career she was good at and loved. Sandy loved working with injured people and loved watching them heal, so going to paralegal school was tough. Because she had to admit that she failed once again, Sandy felt like she was worthless that she could not do anything right.

Paralegal school took a little more than five months to complete. The last four weeks of classes was doing an internship. Sandy chose to do her internship with the courts. Sandy enjoyed working in the courts. She found it to be fun and interesting. Now that school was ending, Sandy had to start looking for a job. Sandy did not know exactly what she wanted to do as a paralegal. Sandy was not sure if she wanted to work in the courts, or for law firm, or even something else, so she spent a few hours a day looking for jobs, sending resumes, and getting reference letters.

About halfway through the course work, Sandy was feeling better so she started to look for a house to buy. It took her about four months, but finally she found the house she wanted. Sandy purchased the house and moved to a small town where she could feel safe. Things moved slowly in the small town. Nikki could walk to school it was only a block away. Sandy graduated from paralegal school in the fall of 1999. She went out looking for work. Sandy found a job two weeks later for a county office. Sandy started working. She was happy that she was back to work. She hated sitting at home. Sandy needed to be busy. She didn't want the depression to come back. Sandy continued to work forty hours a week with her new job and work thirty to thirty-five hours a week at her part-time job.

Within six months, Sandy had her new job down and began working on new projects. Sandy took on many new challenges with work. She constantly wanted to learn more about the government and what they did. She always stayed busy at work, continually asking for more and more to do. The more work she had, the better she felt. It was difficult for her to sit still. Sandy felt she had to keep moving or the depression would come back. When Sandy did not have any work to do, her mind wandered. She hated herself for where she was, and became angry about what she was doing. It was not that she did not like her job; it was not the career she wanted and that made her angry. Sandy had once again failed, as she saw things.

Chapter 13

That spring Sandy's brother moved in with Nikki and her. The following summer Sandy's family came out to visit. They were having a family reunion so they came and stayed for few days, then they all went to the family reunion.

Sandy had always hated going to the family reunions. Sandy never felt like she fit in with the family. She always felt that everyone was looking at her with disappointment. Sandy saw herself as a bad person and did not deserve to be apart of the family.

Sandy came back early because she had to work. Sandy's parents and Nikki came back several days later. The next weekend, Sandy's dad, brother, and friends of the family came over for a cookout. Sandy wanted to show off her house. She wanted to show her family that she was successful, hoping they would stop thinking of her as a failure. Maybe Sandy would stop thinking of herself as a failure. If her family was proud of what she had accomplished, then maybe she would no longer be a failure.

Sandy's dad's, brother and friend of the family were sitting in the garage drinking. Sandy's uncle came into the house to use the bathroom. He saw Nikki on his way back up the stairs. Sandy was in the other room, looking in, holding the dog while her uncle was in the house. He stopped and gave Nikki a hug and patted her on the butt. Sandy went over to talk to her daughter and asked if she was okay, and asked if it felt weird for him patting her on the butt. She did not think that it was bad, but did not really like it. It made Sandy uncomfortable and uneasy. Sandy felt panic, fear, uneasiness, and several other emotions. Part of her thought it was time to fight and protect her; nothing bad was ever going to happen to Nikki if Sandy could help it. Sandy was ready to take action, but she was afraid about what would happen if she did take action. Would her family believe her, would they think she was making it up, would they start looking at Nikki with the same shame with which they looked at her and how could she think she could protect Nikki if she couldn't protect herself when it happened to her?

A few hours later, her uncle went back in the house again to use the bathroom. Sandy went in through the garage door and grabbed the dog. Sandy loved her dog. She was a pure chow and she intimidated people. The dog hated most men, but liked Sandy, Sandy's family and the dog tolerated anybody else who was in the house. The dog was truly a one-family dog. The dog did not like Sandy's uncle from the time he walked into the house. Sandy had to command the dog to stay and not attack. Sandy's uncle did not see her go into the house.

When he came up the stairs Nikki was sitting on the couch watching TV. He went and sat next to her. He leaned over to grab her. Nikki scrunched up into the fetal position, and Sandy walked into the living room with the dog. The dog started barking and growling at him. When he saw Sandy and the dog, he jumped away from Nikki immediately and walked outside. Sandy went up to Nikki and asked if she was okay. She was scared and began to cry. Sandy held her for a while and let her cry on her shoulder. Sandy told her that she would not let her uncle back into the house. The cookout was breaking up. Sandy's mom had walked into the kitchen to start putting things away since everyone was getting ready to leave.

That evening Sandy told her mom what had happened to Nikki. Sandy's mom said how much she had always disliked her uncle and told her about some of the horrible things he had done in the past. It was not the response Sandy was expecting. Sandy wanted her mom to get angry and tell her something comforting. Sandy didn't believe her mom really knew what to say or how to act. Sandy didn't believe that her mom didn't care or wasn't concerned about Nikki and her, she just didn't know what to do or say.

Sex and violence was not something that was talked about by her mom's generation. They were taught to hide. Sexual assault was not something people spoke about. That conversation was taboo. Even when Sandy was a child young adult people did not talk about violence against women. Not until the late '80s early '90s was violence and sexual assault spoken about. The world was changing its views on violence and women. The victims were starting to be recognized not criticized for what happened to them. Not as many people were hiding. People were speaking out. Women were coming forward. Society was starting to change. Blaming the victim slowly started to change and was turning to the violator.

It has not changed completely. We still have a tendency to blame the victim in most situations. By saying things such as, "She shouldn't have been walking alone", "If she wasn't flirting with him, this wouldn't have happened", "She asked for it", "She shouldn't have let him in the home" and "What did she think would happen?"

Sandy was able to be there for Nikki in a way that her parents could never be there for her. Sandy had to protect Nikki from everything she could. Sandy did not want Nikki to ever have to deal with what she did. Sandy wanted Nikki to know that she was there and that she cared, and no matter what happened their relationship would never change. Sandy wanted Nikki to trust her, talk to her, and know that Sandy would always understand and never judge her for her choices.

Chapter 14

A month later, school started and Nikki was now in high school. She was growing up, becoming a young adult. It seemed that she grew up and Sandy didn't notice. Sandy could see the child in her and sometimes she could see the young adult trying to come out. She was trying to break free, yet wanted and needed someone to protect her.

Sandy had started back into therapy after what she believed to be a potential sexual assault on her daughter. Emotions and feelings came flooding back. Sandy had stopped sleeping for days. She only slept during daytime hours. At night she stayed awake, watching and waiting for something to happen. Sandy had trouble controlling her anger. She wanted to lash out, but she couldn't. She could only lash out at herself. When Sandy did lash out, she would become angrier because she was unable to control her anger. Sandy did everything she could to push it back to keep it away. Therapy was a slow start. It took several months to start trusting and opening up to a new therapist. In the first session Sandy explained why she was there, but did not give her many details right away. She did not want to let go. Sandy did not know what would happened if she let go. Sandy was afraid of what might come out, what she would do, how she would react and, most of all, how she would feel and deal with those feelings. Sandy was good at burying feelings. She didn't need to feel anything. It was easier for her to not let anything or anyone touch her enough to get hurt.

As therapy went on that year there were several times Sandy wanted to quit and give up. Sandy didn't think that it was worth her time and effort to go through what was happening to her. At times she thought at any moment the men in the white van were going to come and pick her up and take her away put her in a padded room and throw away the key. Sometimes the pain from the feelings were so bad it made Sandy wish they would come and take her away. In that first year of therapy, there were times that all Sandy wanted was to die. She could have wrecked her car, making it seam like an accident. Sandy couldn't let that happen no matter how much she wanted to. Sandy's instincts for living were stronger than the willingness to die, as were her instinct to protect her daughter from any type of harm. Sandy never wanting Nikki to blame herself or suffer in life in any way. That helped with those moments of desperation that Sandy felt. After about a year, Sandy went to her doctor and was put on antidepressants to help with her mood swings.

When Sandy started back into therapy, she did not know what she was getting herself into. She didn't know what was going to happen. Sandy had to let go of the need to control and let out everything she had spent a lifetime burying. There were times when Sandy wanted to stop therapy. She didn't think she could go any further. Sandy felt it would be better if she was dead. At times, she thought she couldn't handle anything else. At times, Sandy wanted to say that it was not worth the pain, the hurt, the disappointment, anger, and everything else. There were times she would go see the therapist and would want to give up. There were times she felt like she wanted to quit. Many times, Sandy had trouble handling the flood of emotions she was feeling. There were even times when she wanted to start drinking again. Sandy did drink at times and would realize that was not the answer she was looking for. Sandy already knew from drinking before she couldn't find what she needed in a bottle.

The most important thing for Sandy to get out of therapy this time was that she was strong enough to do what she needed to do to finally get over everything. For Sandy, the best thing that could happen was that she would finally deal with all the emotions she was feeling. Sandy knew that she would never get over what had happened to her in the past if she did not deal with those feelings. Sandy knew it was finally time to stop running and deal with her past demons.

Chapter 15

After working as a paralegal for about two years, things were changing for Sandy. Sandy started dating again. Her personal life was going well. Her boyfriend, Jim, and she started talking about marriage.

In 2002, Jim proposed. It took several months to decide on when they were going to get married. Sandy did not know when they should get married. There was just so much to think about when you set the date. When family lives out of town and in other states it makes it even more difficult. They wanted to go on a honeymoon, but did not know where to go so they finally made some decisions about the wedding. It was to be in the spring of 2003. The date picked was the same day of her rape. The people who knew about the rape were surprised that she chose that date. Sandy wanted that day to be a new beginning not a day to run and hide.

Sandy and Jim spent the next several months making plans and deciding what they wanted and didn't want for the wedding. Sandy did not want a big ceremony, something small with select family members and a few friends. They were married in spring of 2003. Sandy had many doubts about getting married. She loved Jim, but she did not know if she could give him what he needed in the relationship. Sandy did not know if she could get what she needed. Jim knew Sandy was in therapy and that things got hard at times. Sandy had a hard time asking or telling people what she needed from them. Sandy put it on herself to make them guess, that way when they were wrong, she could get angry at herself and punish herself even more.

Sandy's emotions were confused. There were times that she would think about calling off the wedding and times that she could not wait for it to happen. Sandy was going through so many emotions that most of the time she did not know which way to go. Sandy was torn between what she felt, what she needed, and what she really wanted. Sandy did want to be with someone for the rest of her life, and she wanted to make her family proud of her. Sandy also wanted to find out who she was, to find out what she really wanted from her life, not what she should do to make everyone else's life come first.

Sandy knew that getting married was the right thing. She finally realized why she was getting married; it was first for herself, second for Jim, and finally for her family. Sandy realized that it was okay to want the same things as other people. Sandy did not have to always be different in the way she thought, acted, or lived. Sometimes it was good to have things in common with other people. Sandy knew that there were other things that made her who she was. It was not just the way she thought, saw things, the way she acted, and the things she did. There was so much more to people. People are all different in some way or another.

The wedding was very nice, small, and intimate with friends and family. The ceremony only took about ten minutes. They went out for dinner and came back to the house for cake.

Chapter 16

Finally, Sandy felt she was doing something right. Finally, she was not a failure. Finally, her family was proud of her. Finally, Nikki had a father. So it seemed. Soon after the wedding Sandy started doubting herself. Did she do this for her family or for herself? The first year she had many doubts. Time went on and she knew that he was right for her and that she wanted to be married to Jim. They had some rough times the first year.

Everyone in the family had to make adjustments. Nikki had a hard time. She was not sure of her place anymore. There was someone else now in the house. Sometimes Sandy thought Nikki wanted him to be a father and other times Nikki was glad he was not her father. He was not sure of his limits with Nikki. Nikki was used to the way things had been and he wanted things a different way. The adjustment to changing habits is difficult for anyone, but I think especially hard for a teenager. She was trying to find out who she was and what she wanted out of life. All of a sudden her life had changed in more ways than one.

Sandy was changing, also, and therapy was helping her find out who she was and what she wanted. Sandy wanted everyone to get along. She wanted everyone to be who they were. Instead, there were times she had to become the peacemaker. Sandy tried to stay out of the way. No matter what she tried to do to keep the peace it did not always work. Sandy did not want to be in the middle of the struggle for power. Nikki was trying to find her place in life. Jim tried to find his place in the family. Sandy was all over the place, not knowing who to support. It is very hard not to choose sides. Jim wanted her to back him up. Nikki wanted her to choose her. Sometimes Sandy was forced to make a choice between arguments. When Sandy would make a choice, she knew that it was not what the other wanted to hear. If Sandy chose Jim, Nikki was hurt. If she chose Nikki, Jim was hurt. So Sandy tried to be objective and make the best decision possible, hear both sides of the story and make a decision. Sometime it worked out okay, other times the person who was not backed up would be mad because Sandy did not choose them. There were things that Jim and Sandy did not agree on. There were times that Nikki was out of line. Since Nikki and Sandy had more of a friendship, when Sandy picked Jim's side she was able to explain why she did what she did. When Sandy picked Nikki's side, Jim understood that Nikki was first in her life. When Sandy would try to explain to Jim why she made that choice he was sometimes too angry to listen, so he went to be by himself for a while. When he felt better about what happened, things would go back to the way they were. Sandy felt guilty about not taking Nikki's side because she only had her in her life. Sandy was the only person that had been there her entire life. Sandy would feel guilty about Jim because he was her husband and she should support him. As time went on they could understand each other a little better. Nikki found her place. Jim was not the father she wanted. They began relating to each other more. Jim found his place as a sometime parent and sometime friend. He found the boundaries he needed. Sandy was in the middle less and less. Not to say things were perfect with the family, but they were working every day to try and respect each other and listen better to the other person. It didn't always work because emotions get in the way, but they were trying. Sandy's role was still the peacemaker, but with each passing day that role vanished more and more.

Nikki was in her final year of high school. Sandy and Jim knew that she would not be out of the house, that she would continue to be with them for a long time, but she would also be becoming more independent as time passed. She would be making more of her own decisions. Right or wrong, they would be the choices she made and she would then have to deal with the outcome. Nikki had really grown over the past two years. She began to realize that she had to make herself happy, and to choose the path based on what she wanted. The only thing Sandy wanted for her was for her to be happy. Nikki had overcome many hurdles in her life. Sandy was proud to call Nikki her daughter. Any choice Nikki made about her life, Sandy would be there to support her no matter what. Nikki had supported Sandy no matter what Sandy had done, even if she was not aware of what she was doing. Nikki never judged Sandy for the choices she made. Sandy would never judge Nikki for the choices she would make in the future. Sandy prayed that when she did make her choices that she made them for herself and not to please her mother or other people in her life. Sandy wanted Nikki to put herself first.

Chapter 17

In the fall 2004, Sandy started going to group therapy. Group therapy was a new experience for Sandy. Sandy had never been in a group with other people who had been sexually assaulted. In the group, everyone had a chance to talk and tell their story and for everyone else find out what happened to them and hear back from the other members of the group. They group met once a week for fifteen weeks. The group took time off around the holidays. The group lasted until 2005.

When the group first started, Sandy was not sure that she should be there. The first meeting was mainly introductions and setting boundaries for the group. The second meeting was trying to figure out what everyone expected to get out of the group. The group was made up of two licensed counselors and six women.

Sandy was not sure that this was the group for her after the third meeting. Sandy had done so much work and she was in a different place than the rest of the women. Sandy had dealt with most of her issues. Sandy needed to get over a few more hurdles. Sandy wanted to stop blaming herself, understand and accept that what happened was not her fault. That there was no way she could have changed things. Some of the women had only just begun with their struggles. Others were in the middle of their journey. Sandy felt she was close to the end of her journey. Sandy wanted to know how she could get something from these people to help her Sandy believed she could say things and look at things that maybe help them, especially since she had already gone through most of her issues.

Group therapy was difficult at times. Sandy had a hard time not only dealing with her rape, but dealing with the emotions the other members brought to the group. Sandy would take their feelings with her after each group meeting. Their story would affect her as much as her own story.

The depression started to worsen. The antidepressants were no longer working. Sandy went to see a psychiatrist. The psychiatrist put Sandy on a new medication. It took her several months to find the right medication. Some medication put Sandy into a deeper depression, causing the mood swings to be even more overwhelming. Other medication had her bouncing off the walls. Sandy was so hyper at times that she couldn't come down from the high it gave her. Finally, the psychiatrist found the right medication and Sandy was feeling better.

Everyone in the group had a chance to talk and tell their story to tell what happened to them and hear back from the other members of the group. For some members of the group it was difficult to tell their story. They would not or could not go into details. Sandy wanted to know details. She wanted to share the details because she wanted to remember what happened, how she felt and what she did or didn't do because, for her, it was her fault that the rape happened. If she could remember and go through the story they could tell her what she could have done differently, if there was something else she could have done. The day came for Sandy to share her story, Sandy got about three quarters of the way through the story. The group was ending for the night and she didn't want to keep people late. Sandy didn't want to inconvenience anyone with keeping them later than usual. Several weeks later as the group was coming to the end of the meetings, Sandy finished her story. That night Sandy realized that she had never said no or asked him to stop. Yes, Sandy fought and struggled, but the words never came out of her mouth; telling him verbally, "NO", "STOP", or "DON'T."

Sandy asked herself why she didn't say any of those words. Why didn't those words come out of her mouth? Maybe if those words came out, then maybe it would not have happened. Is this why she blamed herself for not stopping it from happening? Sandy wondered how many people actually told their attackers, "NO","STOP", "DON'T." Thinking back at that moment, the things on Sandy's mind certainly weren't those words.

Listening to the other people tell their stories helped Sandy to see things that she had beaten herself up over. Believing it was her fault because of what she did that night, walking alone not protecting herself, Sandy always felt the rape was her fault. That she should have known better. This group of people helped her see that walking alone was not wrong and that any person, man, woman or child, has the right to walk alone and be safe.

There were still other reasons Sandy blamed herself, such as not escaping from her attacker and she learned that no matter what she could have done, it could have happened anyway, that if an attacker wants you, he or she will do whatever it takes to get what they want from you. And no one can stop them.

Group therapy was a changing point in Sandy's survival. She learned so much from the people in the group that it helped her to see things that she wouldn't allow herself to see. They shared their stories to help her to see similarities in her own journey and let go of the things that she could not change no matter how hard she wanted to.

Chapter 18

Sandy made some decisions during the beginning of the group. She finally got the courage to send a letter to her parents. She was finally allowing herself to express the feelings about what happened all those years ago, letting her parents know how angry she was at herself, at them, and at the world, telling them how she felt, telling them about feeling that she was a failure, telling them that she never wanted to keep Nikki.

When Sandy's mom received the letter, she called to tell Sandy that she was not disappointed in her and that she was proud of what she had done. She didn't know how she was able to raise Nikki and that she didn't understand that by asking Sandy if she reported the rape it hurt her. Looking back, she realized that she didn't know what to say. She wanted to know what she needed to do for her daughter. She wanted to know if she had to go to court or whatever else needed to be done. As time went on, she wanted to help her daughter, but didn't know how. She said she read books and waited until

Sandy was ready to talk about what happened because that is what she had read to do. She wanted to help, but she didn't know what she could do to help her daughter with this struggle she was going through. Sandy's mom told her that she could talk to her anytime and to call her if she needed anything for her.

A few months later, mother and daughter began writing letters back and fourth. She asked questions about what happened and the things Sandy did. Sandy let her know that if she couldn't answer her questions that she would let her know and that if she wasn't sure she wanted to know, to not ask the question because some things may be hard for her to deal with and to hear.

In the winter of 2005, Sandy became very sick. She had missed the final group meetings. Sandy ended up in the hospital during the last meeting. The group called her the night of the final meeting. Over the past several months they had all shared things that they were afraid of. They worried about how the others would look at them. They were afraid of how they might look to each other. They allowed themselves to share there stories and push the fear aside. Sandy believed that it helped all of them grow. Sandy knew for her that her journey had come to the end. Sandy could see things differently. She could understand things better. It had helped her to finish telling her story. It has helped her to finally be a survivor.

Chapter 19

Sandy was in the hospital two different times in three months. She had developed a staph infection. The doctors could not figure out how she got this or why. At one point they thought she was better. Then three weeks later Sandy was back in the hospital, but this time she was in The ICU for several hours because of a high fever and irregular heartbeat. Sandy spent a total of twelve days in the hospital. Sandy was released from the hospital, and home healthcare was set up. Sandy stayed on the antibiotics for a total of sixteen weeks. Since she became sick and she was unable to work full-time, Sandy was very limited in the amount of time she could work. After being released from the hospital the second time, Sandy spent four weeks at home. She was able to go back to work as soon as the antibiotics were stopped. Sandy could only work half days, because of her low energy level. Sandy worked four hours and was ready for a nap. Sandy's job was not physical, but it was very demanding intellectually and very stressful. Even before she became sick, there were days that a power nap at lunch would rejuvenate her to finish out the day. Now it took longer. It took the rest of the day. She would go home, take a nap and get up in time to make dinner and be ready for bed.

During this time, Sandy was taken off all medications for depression and anxiety. She had stopped going to therapy because she was either too tired to go or not in a good state of mind to want to go. Sandy stopped thinking about the emotional trauma she was going through. She was only thinking about the physical trauma she was going through right then. When Sandy went back to therapy for the first time, all she could talk about was being sick. She was not sure how she was going to make it through this time financially, emotionally, and physically.

While Sandy was in the hospital, they discovered that she was allergic to almost every antibiotic available. Sandy was very limited as to the medications she could take.

The doctors could not figure out why she was so sick. They did not know how she had caught the infection. Over the next several months after the antibiotics ended, Sandy spent time going to immunologists, ear, nose and throat, and arthritis specialists, trying to figure out what had happen to her body and why.

As soon as Sandy stopped taking the antibiotics she would be sick again within days and would have to go back on the antibiotics again. This went on until July. In May, Sandy finally had enough of being sick. She needed to find out what was going on. Sandy found an immunologist who ran a bunch of more tests. She found that she may have Lupus, but she could not confirm it at that time. Sandy started to worry about having Lupus. But having Lupus would not explain the staph infection that kept coming back. So, finally Sandy decided to go to back home where she grew up, hoping that she could find some doctors who could figure out what was going on. The doctors where she lived did not know what was going on. They could only keep her out of the hospital. At the end of July Sandy went to stay with her parents. She had set up appointments to see doctors at the hospital. She had made two appointments. One was with a rheumatologists and the other was with an infectious disease specialist. They reviewed her medical records and had her see a kidney specialist and a dermatologist. They ran more tests. The infectious disease doctor put Sandy on new antibiotics to fight the staph infection. Within two days, they had the test results back and wanted her to come back in for further testing. They had found problems with her kidneys and the possibility of Lupus was becoming more evident. Within a week they had set up for a kidney biopsy. They put her in the hospital overnight to do the biopsy. It would take a couple of weeks for the test results to come back. Sandy went back home to wait for the test results. She had not heard from the doctors in the two weeks so she decided to call and find out about the test results. Sandy found out that she had something called IgA Neuropathy. Sandy would need to go back to her parents' house in three weeks to start treatment. In the fall of 2005, Sandy went back to her parents to see the doctors again. She was put on medication for the IgA and Lupus. After four days of taking the medication she began to get really sick. She was unable to eat. The doctor took her off all medications for a week. Then start again slowly, retaking the medication. When Sandy restarted the antibiotics with the kidney and Lupus medication, the sickness came back. Sandy called the doctors again. They took her off the antibiotics completely. Sandy still was getting sick from the medication occasionally.

Sandy's biggest concern was about being able to work again. How soon would it be before her kidneys failed completely? While Sandy was in the hospital, they discovered that she was allergic to almost every antibiotic available. She was very limited as to what medications she could take. Sandy wondered at times why this hadn't killed her, or if it was going to kill her very slowly. As always, that feeling of wanting to die was in the back of her mind. If she was dead, Nikki would go live with her parent and Jim could go back to his life and the nightmare of her life would finally be over. There were times in the hospital that she hopped she would die. So it would be over. That she would not have to finish her journey and if she died in the hospital, Nikki would not blame herself for her death as she did not cause it to happen. That it was medical and she could not do anything to change that. Jim would go back to the way his life was before Sandy came into it. He would be a little sadder and angrier because she was gone, but he would be able to move on with his life. Nikki would be able to move on with her life, knowing that her mom loved her the best she could and that she would always be cared for. Her family would make sure she would get what she needed. As for Sandy dying, all the bad things that happened in her life would be over and she would no longer have to deal with the pain, shame, anger, fear, guilt, disappointment, and all the other bad feelings she still had inside. Since death did not happen, the family was back to its daily events. Sandy would have to complete her journey of healing.

Sandy continued with working on the emotions she kept inside. She was finally able to let go of them. After becoming sick, she new that she had to let them go. Sandy knew that someday she would die because everybody dies, but Sandy also knew that she needed to move past all the old emotions. She knew she needed to make the best of the time she had left.

Sandy wondered how much more she would have to endure in her life. Sandy sometimes wondered why her life happened this way, why she was the one who had to keep fighting? First, the rape, then a child, then the robbery, and everything else she had to deal with and now a disease.

Sandy has not gone into remission, but she is hopeful that someday she will. She has decided that until that day comes, she is going to do everything she can to make herself happy, no matter what the cost.